I0557940

Desires of the Heart

a novel

TIFFANY S. DORAN

Fiery Autumn Publishing

Printed in the United States of America
First Printing, 2023

ISBN-13 (Trade Paperback): 979-8-9881818-0-4
ISBN-13 (eBook): 979-8-9881818-1-1

Fiery Autumn Publishing

Learn more about the author at www.tiffanysdoran.com.

ACKNOWLEDGMENTS

First, I would like to thank God for his encouragement as I worked on this book. I thank him for all the ways he inspired me in this endeavor and for putting all the right people in my path as I wrote. I also thank him for giving me the mind I have, that of a writer.

Thank you to my husband for his never-ending support on this journey. We have shared a lot in our lives and I'm glad we can share this as well. Thank you for your love and patience as we climbed this mountain together.

To my children, your prayers and support have meant so much. Thanks for sticking with me.

A big thank you to my extended family for their prayers and support as well, and for believing in this dream. We did it.

I'd also like to thank my virtual writing coach and mentor, Timothy Pike. He pushed me every day with blog posts, e-mails, and writing challenges to do my best and complete this novel.

Thank you to everyone who had a part in making this dream a reality!

Desires of the Heart

CHAPTER ONE

Love or Lust

"I wondered if you were going to be joining me," Katie Calhoun said, smiling at her father as he sauntered into the kitchen. He looked worn out. "Breakfast is ready, Daddy, and I poured you a nice, hot cup of joe."

"Thank you, Peach. I'm starving," Randy Calhoun said as Katie set his plate on the table. He sat down and took a bite. "What would I do without you?"

Even though it was a rhetorical question, Katie knew the answer: he would fix himself a bowl of instant oatmeal and be done with it. But seeing him dig right in to those two thick pieces of French toast, which she had carefully placed one on top of the other with melting butter, a drizzle of syrup, and a dusting of powdered sugar, it was clear how grateful he was for her cooking.

Katie sat down with her own plate and looked over at her dad. Usually, he'd come down for an early breakfast, dressed for a long day on the farm and looking lively. But today, she was pretty sure he'd just run a comb through his hair and splashed some water on his face after waking up late. Now that she thought about it, he'd been doing this more and more in recent months.

It was possible he'd spent a sleepless night thinking about the fire again. Two years ago, almost everything he owned had been destroyed when a massive blaze tore across the farm. Even though insurance covered everything, rebuilding was hard, and the whole ordeal had taken its toll on him. He wasn't even fifty, but his previously dark brown hair was starting to gray, and around his eyes—which were still a brilliant blue—wrinkles were appearing.

"Welp, time to get these chores done," Randy said, pushing his plate away. There'd be no time to dawdle over coffee this morning. He glanced at his watch. "Where is Buck? He's usually here by now."

A knock at the front door answered the question and gave Katie instant butterflies in her stomach. *Surely that was him.* She jumped up and glanced down the long, narrow hallway that led to the front door. Her heart raced faster seeing his sizable yet slim silhouette through the decorative paned-glass windows. She would know it anywhere: broad shoulders, trim waistline, cowboy hat.

Katie paused for a few seconds to arrange her hair, then pulled the door open, letting the warm, mid-May sun pour into the foyer of the farmhouse and spill down the hardwood floor to the living room. Against the bright light, there he stood: William Buck Brady, six feet one, muscular build, dark hair, beautiful smile. In her eyes, the most handsome farmhand her daddy had ever brought on.

"Reporting for duty, ma'am," Buck said, grinning and tipping his hat.

Katie giggled. "Come in, Buck. Would you like a cup of coffee before work?"

"Maybe a quick one," he said, following Katie to the kitchen. "We're off to a late start this morning."

That Buck liked Katie was no secret—he'd been asking her for a date for almost the entire three years he'd worked there. But every time he asked, she turned him down.

In truth, Katie liked him too. She thought she might even love him. But her daddy would never allow the relationship to happen. "You're my pride and joy, Peach," Randy would explain whenever the subject of Buck came up. "You're my only daughter. You were my rock when I thought I was going to lose it all." Katie wasn't exactly sure why that meant she couldn't date Buck, but she suspected her father's biggest fear was marrying her off and losing her for good.

"Did you hear about the county fair that's coming through town?" Buck asked, taking a sip of his coffee.

"Really? I just love fairs!" Katie's eyes lit up.

She remembered going many times as a child, staying for hours just to listen to music and people-watch. But the best part of fairs had to be the food. Every single time, they would find themselves at the dessert stand ordering peach cobbler, and the kind lady who ran the booth knew Katie and prepared it just the way she liked it: perfectly golden-brown peaches, extra-crispy crumble, and a gigantic scoop of vanilla ice cream on top. Watching his little girl devour her outsized dessert, Randy always told her she was going to turn into a peach someday. And in a way she did: one day he called her Peach, and the name stuck.

But it had been such a long time since they'd been to a county fair—or had had any fun for that matter. The fire saw to it that any enjoyable activities would have to wait until things were re-established. But now, as life returned to normal … why *couldn't* they go?

"We should go," Randy declared. He must have read her mind. "Buck, do you happen to remember when the fair will be arriving?"

Katie looked over at Buck. His dark-hazel eyes caught the light of the sun, entrancing her all over again. She knew she shouldn't dream about him the way she did, but she couldn't control it. About the only thing she could do was not let Buck know how she felt, and certainly not let her father know how head over heels she was. But in private, she longed for his touch on her face, his breath on her neck, his lips on hers.

"… right, Katie?" Buck's voice sounded far away as she came out of her daydream.

"Sorry, what was that?"

"I said I reckon the fair would be on a weekend here soon, and I'm sure it won't take much to convince you to go. Right?" Buck grinned.

"Exactly right," Katie said, standing up to clear the dishes. "Well, gentlemen, this work ain't gonna do itself, and those chickens are getting louder by the second wanting their feed."

Randy glanced at his watch. "Yeah, I guess you're right, Peach." He gave Buck a firm pat on the back. "Let's get out there, buddy."

Today, like most days, was sunny and hot, and for the men, the chores were endless: feed the animals, clean the stalls, gather the eggs, milk the cows. That afternoon, Katie found herself staring out the kitchen window at Buck as he loaded hay onto her dad's pickup truck. His shirtless chest glistened in the heat, and she couldn't stop a smile from tickling the corners of her mouth thinking about how romantic it would be to watch the stars at the county fair, his arms wrapped around her waist, her head on his shoulder, a love song playing in the background. She was so lost in her thoughts, she didn't notice her dad had wandered away from the truck.

"Hey, Peach."

She whirled around to see Randy walking in. "Whew, you scared me, Daddy," she said.

"My, my, what are we thinking about so intensely there, darlin'?"

"Oh, it's nothing dad, you know me." She shrugged. "I get lost in my own world at times."

"Well, if that answer helps you sleep better at night, Peach, I guess I'll have to agree with you." Randy threw her the side-eye and smiled.

Opening a cabinet, he grabbed two glasses and filled them with ice. Then he set them on the counter and poured them full of lemonade.

He took a long drink and wiped his brow. Buck came into the kitchen just then, and Randy held out one of the glasses for him.

"Thank you, Randy. You really spoil me with this fresh-squeezed lemonade every day."

Katie couldn't help but smile. She didn't know why she was smiling. All he did was say he appreciated the lemonade.

Randy noticed her smile and cast a glance her way. She cleared her throat and walked to the refrigerator to fix herself a cold glass of peach tea.

Over the years, Katie's love of peach cobbler had grown into a love of peach iced tea, and she'd developed the perfect recipe: fresh-brewed tea, lots of ice, and just the right amount of peach simple syrup. Sometimes, she would even cut a thin slice of peach and place it on the rim of the glass to make it look fancy.

She took a sip. "Well, if you will excuse me, gentlemen, I've got laundry to tend to." Iced tea in hand, she walked out, humming a little tune.

That Saturday, Katie was making her way to Merriman's Fresh Market to pick up a few things when she spotted the sign for the county fair hanging on a storefront window:

COME ONE, COME ALL
TO THE FAIR OF A LIFETIME!
RIDES, MUSIC, FIREWORKS,
FINGER-LICKIN' FOOD
PIG RACING AND PETTING ZOO
FOR THE KIDDOS
AND NEW THIS YEAR: DANCING!

Only one more week, she thought. *I can't wait*. Distracted by thoughts of how much fun she was surely going to have, she continued on her way to Merriman's.

Tink-a-tink-tink, went the bell over the door.

"Good morning, Katie!" Frank Merriman said as she walked in. "It's great to see you." Frank always greeted his customers with a smile and a cheerful tone. He'd owned that store as far back as she could remember.

Mid-fifties, broad at the shoulders but lean at the hips, dark hair starting to gray around his sideburns, Frank had always insisted on being called by his first name. He said it made things more personal, and Katie agreed. What's more, there was a softness in his eyes that always made her feel welcome and wanted. "What'll it be for you today, young lady?" he asked.

"Oh, I'm just here to pick up a few odds and ends is all," she said, smiling.

"Flowers, too, I'm sure." He winked. "Well, you just let me know if I can help you with anything," he said as Katie made her way into the store.

Like most days, her first stop was the floral counter, which she loved because of the eye-popping assortment of colors—reds, yellows, purples, blues—that always jumped out to entice her. For Katie, keeping fresh flowers in the house was a point of pride. They filled the whole place with a sweet aroma, and almost made her feel like she was living in a garden.

She picked out a lovely bouquet of lilacs, gathered a few items for that night's meal, then headed for the checkout at the front of the store.

"Hey, Katie."

Tate Stevens had stepped out right in front of her from behind a shelf.

"Oh my gosh, you scared me," she said, holding her hand over her chest. "Hi there."

He stared back at her. Tall and thin with shoulder length, wiry brown hair, Tate always appeared slightly disheveled. And his sunken eyes made him look like he hadn't slept in days.

Katie wasn't quite sure what to say. "Um, are you having a good day, Tate?"

"Yes." He paused, then shifted his stance a little. "I mean, I am now." He continued to stare at her. Then he smiled.

He does have a nice smile, Katie thought. *And he is so sweet to me whenever he sees me.* Still, she couldn't shake the feeling that something was off about him. But she told herself he was just quiet and socially awkward and left it at that.

"Well," she said, "I guess I better get going before everything hits the floor. I knew I should've used a basket." She clutched her armful of groceries tighter and kept going toward the front of the store. She could feel Tate's stare as she walked away.

"Will this be all for you today?" Frank asked.

"Yes, that'll do it for today." Katie laid her items on the counter and reached into her purse to grab her wallet.

Tink-a-tink-tink!

Katie turned around to see who had come in. There he was: Buck Brady, in all his handsome glory. He had on his white Stetson cowboy hat, plaid white-and-blue shirt with the top two buttons open, and blue jeans that would make any girl get carried away with her imagination. Not to mention a smile that lit up his face and matched his chiseled jawline. Her heart pounded, and she tried to compose herself. After all, Buck worked for her dad, and she couldn't let on that she liked him. The heat in her cheeks made her wonder if Frank—or worse, both of them—suspected anything.

"Well, well, if it isn't Miss Katie Calhoun," Buck said, flashing those perfectly straight, white teeth.

Katie couldn't count the number of times she'd dreamed about being close enough to taste his lips and find out if he was as sweet to the tongue as he was to the eye.

"Y-yes. I'm, I—" She saw Buck almost every day, yet here she was, a stammering mess. "I'm just here for a few things and, um, some flowers for the house." Feeling her cheeks flush again, she paid Frank as quickly as she could and made a beeline for the door.

She didn't know what it was about him that made her feel like a schoolgirl again. Maybe the way he looked at her, or something about his smile. Whatever it was, she was powerless against it. Their eyes met as she moved past him on her way to the door, and her knees went weak. She managed a brief goodbye, then walked out.

❧

From inside, Buck watched as Katie made her way across the parking lot, then turned to Frank. "There's something about her, Frank. Something I just can't put my finger on."

"But I'm sure it's something you want to know, isn't it, Buck?" Frank said with a wink.

Buck smiled. "You know it, Frank. You know it."

He watched her walk all the way to the truck and pull away before starting his shopping. As he passed the flowers, he thought of Katie. They paled in comparison to her beauty: her bright green eyes, auburn curls that fell loosely around her shoulders, that gorgeous, innocent smile. He wasn't sure she felt that way about him, though. He was nearing twenty-five, and she would be twenty-two in the fall. And for the last three years, she had rejected all his advances. Still, he couldn't stop thinking about her.

∽

Back at the house, Katie prepared dinner. Vegetables, fresh from the garden and steamed to perfection, seared lamb on a bed of white rice, and her prize-winning blueberry pie for dessert. She spread out a tablecloth and placed the lilacs in the center of the table. Lilacs, she thought, were the perfect fit for this evening's meal. And it would be a meal for a king tonight.

Sure, she spoiled her daddy, but that was okay. He worked long hours, every single day. She could see on his face he was tired of dealing with the continual stress of farm living and wished he could just relax and retire. Wake up every day, sit out on the front porch in his favorite rocker, drink his coffee, read the paper, and not have to worry about the pressures of everyday life. He was getting older, and just as he had cared for her since she was born, Katie wanted to finally be able to do that for him.

"My, my, what have we got here?" her dad asked as he came into the kitchen. "I could smell it from the barn and figured it must be time for supper." He made his way to the sink to wash his hands.

"You're just in time," Katie said, pouring two glasses of red wine. "I hope you brought your appetite."

Randy dried his hands off. "This looks amazing, Peach. Let's pray so we can dig in."

They discussed many topics over dinner that night, such as the fair that was coming and all the fun they were going to have trying different foods and watching the pigs race. Then her dad changed the subject, and completely threw her for a loop.

"Look, Peach," Randy said, lowering his tone. "I've been watching you, and I think it's time you found someone. Someone to love you and take care of you. You're a beautiful girl, and you need someone to spoil you and show you life outside of this here farm."

"Daddy, you're being silly," Katie replied with a chuckle. "I have all of that here already. You love me and take care of me and spoil me. I don't need to leave the farm for that."

But he had a point. She, too, wanted a man who loved her. For a moment she considered telling her dad how much she wanted that man to be Buck Brady, but quickly thought better of it. "Maybe someday my prince will come, Daddy, but for right now, this is all I need." She smiled as she stood up from the table. "Now, how about some pie?"

The freshly made blueberry pie sat cooling on the counter, and steam slowly rose as she cut into it. She placed a hearty slice on a plate, sprinkled some powdered sugar on top, and sat it in front of her dad along with a piping hot mug of coffee.

"You know," Randy said, taking his first bite, "I changed my mind. Maybe you do have everything you need here." He laughed. Katie winked at him, squeezed his shoulder, then walked to the sink.

She had just pulled her hair back to start washing dishes when they heard a sharp knock on the front door. They looked at each other, wondering who it could be. Randy took a quick sip of his coffee then stood up to answer the door.

"Well, I'll be!" Randy exclaimed from the front hall. "This night is full of surprises. Come on in! We were just finishing dinner." His voice got louder as he entered the kitchen. "Peach, look what the cat dragged in!"

Katie turned from the sink and almost dropped the glass she had just finished washing.

CHAPTER TWO

The Past in the Present

For a few seconds, Katie thought she might faint. There in the kitchen doorway stood someone she didn't think she'd ever see again: Matthew Fuller. Yet there he was, dressed much the way she remembered: ball cap, jeans, and a light-blue pullover. His style hadn't changed at all. Matt took off his hat and held it against his chest as he entered the kitchen.

She couldn't believe it was him. Four years ago, when they were both seventeen, she and Matt had been in a relationship. Some would call it puppy love, but she ... she had it all planned out. They would be married during the summer months in the barn that her mom and dad had built. The reception would be held in the large, fenced-in backyard. Instead of a "Just Married" sign on the back of a car, she wanted them to be riding horses, each tied to the other by a rope, with a sign hanging between them that read, "Just Hitched." Yet this elaborate wedding would only be a formality—in her mind, they were already married.

Randy cleared his throat, snapping her out of her trance.

Katie quickly regained her composure and walked over to greet him with a hug. "How are you, Matt?" she asked, running her trembling fingers through her hair. Her mouth had gone dry, her heart raced. "I mean, have you been doing well? I mean, what brings you to our neck of the woods?" She tried to calm her nerves, but her thoughts were all over the place.

"Matt, why don't you have a seat," Randy said, pulling a chair out from the table.

"Sure, thank you." Matt set his hat on the table and sank his tall, slender frame into the chair.

Katie couldn't help but stare at him. She leaned against the refrigerator, taking in every curve of his face, his blond hair, his crystal-blue eyes. Just his presence made her feel safe and helped her calm down. Matt had been there for them during the horrible fire, and now, all it took was his scent to bring the memories rushing back.

It had been an unusually dry summer. Several loads of hay sat outside, waiting to be taken to the barn. At that moment, someone flicked a

9

cigarette out the window of a passing car, and … *poof!* It was all gone. The barn that her parents had spent months building, reduced to cinders. The fence posts Randy so painstakingly dug into the ground, charred like burnt matchsticks. The fire had ruined it all.

Thankfully, their church had donated plenty of items to help them through. But the fire happened just after her mother, Abigail, had been killed in a drunk-driving accident, and it broke Katie's heart to see her father standing there surveying the smoldering farmland. Katie knew how much the farm meant to him, and now he had to experience loss all over again. Many of her mom and dad's memories were made in that barn, and now it was nothing but ashes and soot.

Matt and his family stepped up, coming out to the farm almost every day to help clean up and rebuild. She loved it when he showed up. She felt so safe and warm in his arms. His scent was her security, and she didn't feel as empty with him around.

But one day, everything changed. Katie ran to greet him as she always did, longing for that safe feeling. She gave him a big hug. Then he looked into her eyes and her world fell apart.

"Katie, I don't know how to tell you this, but Mom and I, we're …" Matt's voice quavered, and he hesitated for a moment. "We're moving."

"Moving?" Katie scanned his face, looking for any sign he was teasing, but instead saw tears welling in his eyes. She had to choke back her own tears to continue. "Where would you move to, Matt?"

"California," he said. "Mom got a promotion, and it's a mand—" He paused. "It's a mandatory relocation."

Katie couldn't hold the tears back any longer. She covered her face and sobbed into her hands.

"Don't cry, Katie. Please, don't cry. I didn't know when or how to tell you." A tear rolled down his cheek. "With everything going on here there really wasn't a right time."

Katie wiped away her own tears with the back of her hand. "When do you have to go?"

"It'll be a couple of months yet. We still have to pack up and sell our home, but Mom thinks she's already found us a place there." As he spoke, Katie wrapped her arms around his waist and held him as tightly as she could.

On the day Matt left, the sun was covered by gray clouds, and the wind blew cold. The day felt much as her heart did.

"I love you, Katie. With every fiber in me, I love you." She held him

10

for as long as she could. Almost as if the longer she held him, the longer he would be in her life, her heart, her presence. He kissed her long and hard, with more passion than any kiss she could remember.

Katie stood on her front porch and watched him drive off until she could no longer see his taillights. Until she was sure she wouldn't see his truck slow to a stop and him running back to her. Then she went up to her room, threw herself across the bed, and cried.

Now, here he was in her kitchen, standing right in front of her. She couldn't believe it. "Would you like a drink, Matt?" She reached into the fridge for her pitcher of iced tea.

"No thanks, Kat. I can't stay long." *Kat. Wow, I haven't been called that since the day he left.* Hearing it again brought her a sense of ease, and she started to relax.

"So, Matt, what brings you out here again?" Randy asked.

Matt smiled. "Well, a friend of mine wants to move out here, and I offered to come along and give him the grand tour since I grew up here. We'll be staying at his parents' house." He stood up from the table and grabbed his hat. "I was going to wait to stop by until tomorrow seeing as how it's late, but I'm glad I didn't." He winked at Katie, and she felt her cheeks flushing.

"Well, when you're not too busy showing your friend around," Randy said, "feel free to stop by again before you go."

"By the way, Matt," Katie said, "the fair is in town this weekend. Will you still be here for that?"

"I wouldn't miss it." Matt grinned and tipped his hat her way. Then he shook Randy's hand. "Goodnight, sir."

As the door closed behind him, she felt as if a door had opened again in her heart. She went upstairs to her bedroom window. She pulled back her lacy, white curtains and watched him climb into his truck and drive off, just as she had all those years before.

The next morning, excitement filled Katie's heart as she headed downstairs to fix coffee and breakfast. The sun was shining through the kitchen window, and she couldn't stop herself from humming.

Her dad walked in. "What has you so happy this morning, Peach?"

"Oh, you know," she said, "the fair, the sun—"

"Matt?" Randy winked at her.

Katie looked down and blushed. "Maybe a little. But—" She was interrupted by a knock at the front door.

"I reckon that would be Buck," Randy said. "Why don't you run

11

and open that door, and I'll finish getting our cups of coffee together." He walked over to the coffee bar.

Buck Brady! How could I have forgotten about him? Katie's mind whirled as she made her way down the hall to let him in. *Matt and Buck, Matt and Buck. Boy, oh boy, what am I going to do?*

❧

Buck greeted Katie with a smile and a hug, then followed her to the kitchen.

"Buck, look out!" Randy yelled. Before he could even realize what he was doing, Buck had walked straight into the wall next to the kitchen doorway.

Katie wheeled around. "Oh my gosh, Buck, are you okay?" She reached out to touch his shoulder.

"I'm fine, you guys, I just ..."

"What's got your mind so busy this morning, Mr. Brady?" Randy said.

Well, sir, I'm head over heels in love with your daughter and I'm a complete basket case around her, he wanted to say. But he didn't want to reveal that right now, even though he could no longer deny that his feelings for Katie were getting stronger. And lately, he'd been feeling more frazzled than ever in her presence.

So instead, he searched his mind for an excuse. "Uh, well, Randy, y-you know ..." *Think, Buck!* "You know ... coffee. Um, you see, I ... haven't had any yet, and I-I guess I'm not fully awake," he said. "I'm sure I'll be fine once I, you know, have some coffee." Wow, did he ever feel like an idiot.

Later that afternoon, as he and Randy took a break, Buck looked up to see Katie walking down the hill from the house. What a beautiful sight she was. He thought back to when he started working at the farm, three years ago. She had matured so much since then. But it was more than her looks that made her attractive. It was her mind, her heart, her soul. And she was such a good girl, taking care of Randy and making sure he had everything he needed. *But what about her?* Buck wondered. *Does she have everything she needs?*

"Hey, pretty lady!" he yelled as she got closer.

Katie waved and flashed a huge smile. "Hello! Are you working hard down there or are you hardly working?"

Buck grinned. "What do you think?" he said, wiping his sleeve across his forehead.

"Why don't you two take a break and come in for some lemonade?"

"You sure do have good timing, Peach," Randy said. "I was just thinking how good that would be right about now."

∽

They sat and talked over lemonade for a little while, then Randy and Buck went back outside while Katie stayed in the kitchen. A few minutes later, there was a knock at the door. Katie wasn't expecting anyone, but she got up and made her way down the front hallway. She instantly recognized the outline of the person standing there: Matt Fuller. As if on cue, the memories came flooding back, but she put on a big smile anyway and opened the door.

"Matt, it's so nice to see you!" she said. "Dad's out back. Why don't we go say hi?"

As they walked down the hill, Katie fixed her gaze across the expansive farm and its endless rows of corn. She remembered how tall she used to think the corn was when she was a young girl. It looked almost as if it would reach all the way up into the heavens. Life on a farm, as she saw it, was the best life to have. The cows grazing in the field, the pigs nosing in the mud, and the horses trotting around the enclosure Randy and Buck had built last summer all brought a smile to her face, and she felt so blessed to live there.

Randy's face lit up when he saw them approaching. "Hey, Matt!" he said. "I'm glad you came back."

Buck, who was standing off to the side, nodded and gave Matt a half smile.

"Where are my manners," Katie said. "Matt, this is Buck Brady. He's been a great friend of ours for years. He's Daddy's right-hand man."

Buck walked over to Matt and shook his hand. "So, you used to live here as well, I hear?"

"Yeah, I lived up the road a little ways," Matt said. "Katie and I used

13

to date back in high school."

"Ahh. I see, I see," Buck said.

Katie sensed some tension, and it made her feel awkward. Fortunately, her dad diffused the situation by offering to show Matt around the newly fixed-up farm.

"Come with me, Matt," Randy said. "Let's go take a look at that barn. It looks a lot different than when you saw it last."

Katie told Buck she'd see him later, then walked back up to the house, glad she could finally breathe a little easier with the guys distracted. She went to the living room and plopped down on the oversized, brown-suede sofa. She grabbed a pillow, hugged it tightly against her, and sighed, wondering what she should do.

Through a tangle of emotions, she didn't quite know what to feel. Of course, she liked Buck a lot and would date him in a heartbeat. And visions of them having fun at the fair together ran through her mind constantly. But then Matt showed up. Matt ... of all people! The man she wanted to marry and spend the rest of her life with years ago. She let out a big sigh, blowing a stray piece of hair out of her face.

"What do I do, Momma?" Katie asked, looking over at the framed picture of her mom near the grandfather clock in the corner. Her smile was so soft, and she remembered her touch was, too. She tried to think what her mom would tell her to do.

At that moment, Randy walked into the living room. She hadn't heard him come in, but she was glad he was there. His handsome face gave her so much comfort. "Oh, Daddy, I'm stuck," she said. "I feel torn between my past love and, well ..." She paused, not wanting to tell him about her feelings for Buck.

"Oh, you mean how you feel about Buck, Peach?"

She looked at him, puzzled and surprised, as he walked over to the couch. "You ... you mean, you know?"

"I can read you like a book, honey." Randy sat down beside her. "Look, who says you have to do anything with either of them right now? Who says you have to make a choice? I think you're putting too much pressure on yourself. Matt just got here, and he won't be here for long. You also would have to get to know him as he is now, because you only remember the Matt from years ago."

"I guess you're right, Daddy," she said, then sighed. "I just never thought it would be this difficult."

"Well, love is a precious thing, and sometimes, you have to fight for

14

it." He rubbed her cheek. "Whatever your decision is later on, I know it'll be the right one."

Randy patted her knee and stood up. "Oh, and as far as what your momma would do? She would just stick with me," he said, chuckling.

Katie chuckled too. She needed that. And he was right. She shouldn't be overloading herself with all of this. She wasn't committed to either one of them. Why couldn't she just take some time to get to know both a little better? Buck on a deeper, personal level and Matt for who he was now.

Later that evening, as Matt got ready to leave, Katie walked him out to his truck. The night was clear, and the stars glistened in the sky.

"Sure is a beautiful night," Katie said as she looked up to the sky. "The stars are so bright."

Matt reached for her hand. "Not quite as bright as the stars in your eyes, Katie."

She looked over at him, nudging his arm and laughing. "You're such a romantic. Some things never change."

He took her hand in his. "There's a lot that hasn't changed, Katie," he said. "I've missed you so much."

She'd wanted to hear that for so long. But now, it just confused her even more.

Katie looked into his eyes. "I've missed you too, Matt." But she couldn't shake the feelings that had arisen since seeing him again. *Are these old feelings or new ones?* she wondered. It was probably the first answer, if she were being honest with herself. But as she was processing how to feel, he leaned closer, cupped her face gently in his hands, and kissed her. That kiss was even more passionate than the one he had given her before moving away. She felt dizzy from it, and a little scared. But she also felt ... love. Could it be, though? Her next thought came through loud and clear: *Could he still love me after all these years?*

Before he headed upstairs for the night, Randy glanced out the window just in time to see Matt kiss Katie. "Oh, Peach," he said out loud. "Guard her heart, dear Lord. Please."

15

A few minutes later, he heard Katie open the front door and lock it behind her. On his way upstairs, he passed by the living room and saw her lying on the sofa, hugging the same pillow, already asleep in front of the dwindling fire. Randy covered her with a blanket, put out the fire, and called it a night.

CHAPTER THREE

Love Hurts

The next morning, the rays of sun through the huge bay window of the living room hit Katie directly in the face, refusing to let her sleep. This was followed by footsteps on the stairs and down the hallway as her dad shuffled into the kitchen. She *really* didn't want to get up today. Pulling the blanket over her head, Katie vowed to boycott the day by not getting off the couch at all. Unfortunately, her bladder had other plans, and the smell of fresh coffee filling the room also helped change her mind.

As Katie brushed her teeth, another familiar aroma perked her up: her dad's Roadhouse Omelets. "Yes! Dad is cooking," she said out loud. Roadhouse Omelets were a family favorite. For Katie, they were the perfect blend of eggs, cheese, peppers, and onions. She made a beeline for the kitchen.

On the table sat a steaming cup of coffee, a plate with an omelet, and two slices of toast with apple butter and jelly on the side.

"You know, Daddy, I could get used to this," she said, smiling over the rim of her coffee cup as she took a sip. Randy sat down beside her, said a blessing over the food, and they both dug in. Her dad didn't cook often, but when he did, it was delicious. She ate every bite on her plate, then poured herself another cup of coffee.

"So, the fair is in a couple of days, huh?" Randy asked.

"Sure is!" Katie smiled.

Randy's cell phone rang from the living room. He got up to answer it while Katie took their dishes to the sink. As she glanced out the window, her attention was captured by the activity of the farm: the foals in the enclosure running around, the pigs eating their slop, and the cows being let out to graze.

The cows being ... wait, who is letting the cows out? she thought. *Buck isn't even here yet!* Just then, a man she didn't know came into view. *Who on Earth is that?*

"Daddy!" she yelled. "There is a strange man in the field letting our cows out!"

Randy walked in from the living room, still on the phone.

"Okay, Buck, that sounds good. See you later." Her dad didn't sound all that concerned.

"That's our new helper for the day, Peach. Buck isn't feeling well today, so he asked a friend to come over and help out. That was Buck on the phone just now, calling to make sure he had shown up."

Katie placed her hand on her forehead. "Whew, that scared me to death. I thought someone was stealing our cows." She frowned. "What's wrong with Buck?"

"I think it's just a twenty-four-hour thing. I'm sure he'll be back on his feet in no time."

"I hope so. We're supposed to go to the fair in a few days."

Just before evening, Katie headed into town and stopped by Merriman's Fresh Market to grab some flowers for the house and soup and crackers for Buck to help raise his spirits. The flowers on display were so beautiful. They were almost as beautiful as the ones they had growing at their home. But instead of picking them, Katie and her mom always bought them from Merriman's. Her mom said she didn't like the idea of plucking a thriving life from the garden just to put it in a vase when there were already flowers that had been picked for that purpose. She also said it would be a waste of flowers if someone didn't buy them.

As she walked in, Katie was greeted first by the smell of coffee beans and blueberry muffins, then by Frank's cheerful voice.

"There she is! We just got some fresh flowers in today, Katie, and they are gorgeous."

She smiled. "I'll be sure to check them out. Thank you, Frank."

She made her way to the soup aisle and picked up some chicken noodle soup and crackers before making a quick stop by the floral department to check out the new arrivals. The flowers were as beautiful and vibrant as Frank had promised. Bright-pink roses and blue-and-yellow lilies almost called out to her as she stood deciding what to get. For Buck, she settled on the lilies, and for their home, the roses, which would be the perfect centerpiece for the kitchen table.

"Uh-oh, who is feeling down?" Frank asked, noticing the soup and crackers as Katie set her items on the counter. He furrowed his eyebrows. "It's not your dad, is it?"

"No, he's doing great. These are for Buck. He's feeling under the weather today, and I thought this would help him feel better."

Frank placed everything into a bag and smiled. "Well, I'm sure just seeing you will be all the help he needs," he said with a wink. His comment left her confused, but she smiled anyway, picked up her shopping bag, and said goodbye.

Just before dusk, she arrived at Buck's place and drove up the long, winding dirt driveway. She parked, walked past the manicured bushes, just as the crickets began to chirp, and then onto the covered front porch where rocking chairs swayed in the breeze. She knocked on the door. For almost a minute she stood waiting. Just as she raised her hand to knock again, the door swung open. There stood Buck, unshaven, wearing a pair of loose-fitting, gray sweatpants and no shirt.

He looked surprised. "Katie, hey," Buck said, running his hand through his disheveled hair. "Please, come in. But don't get too close just in case I'm contagious."

He looks good even when he's sick, she thought as she followed him into the kitchen. She set the soup and crackers on the counter. "I brought you some things to help you feel better."

"Aww. Thanks, hon," Buck said, slipping on a tee shirt. "That was sweet."

Katie stepped away from the counter and moved toward the living room, where Buck had a roaring fire going. Her shoes click-clacked on the shiny hardwood floor as she walked over to his brown-leather sofa.

"Here, let me move my pillow and quilt so you can sit down. As you can see, I've been napping all day." He almost sounded embarrassed.

Katie patted the sofa next to her for him to sit down. "So, how are you feeling?"

"I felt really sluggish and tired this morning, and my nose was stuffy." He sat down and laid his arm on the back of the couch. "But now that I've slept, I feel much better."

"Well, that's great to hear, because you and I have a date for the fair soon."

"Wow! A date, huh?" He winked.

Did I just say that? She had gotten so carried away with her thoughts that she actually called it a date.

"Well, you ... you know what I mean," she stammered. "Not like a date, date. More like a ... you know—"

"Of course, not a date, date." He chuckled. "No worries, you've turned me down for all three years that I've worked for your dad anyway."

His comment made Katie feel awkward, but she knew he didn't mean to make her feel that way. Instead of replying, she gave him a big smile and stood up.

"Well, I guess I better get. I don't want dad worrying about me."

"Okay. Please tell him I should be there in the morning." Buck stood up and wrapped his arms around her.

She hugged him back. Then, ever so slowly, they pulled away from one another until her arms slid down to his waist, and all they could hear were the other's lustful breaths. She looked up at him. He gazed deep into her emerald-green eyes.

"Katie," he whispered. "If you don't move right now, I'll be forced to kiss you."

The fire behind them sent a mysterious glow dancing across Buck's chiseled features. *He's so beautiful,* she thought. Her legs were jelly, and whether he realized it or not, he was holding her up. She had dreamed of being this close to him, being right here in this spot with him. His breath on her face, his lips on hers.

He leaned in and cupped his strong, tanned hands around her face. Her stomach twisted itself into knots and her body tingled with antic-ipation. But she stopped him.

"Buck, I can't," she whispered as she leaned her forehead onto his.

Buck sighed. She knew this was hard for him to hear. It was hard for her, too.

"I'm sorry, Buck. I'll get sick, and as you know, the fair is this week-end. I just don't want to risk it." She winked and laughed.

"Are you kidding me?" Buck tried to compose himself.

"Aww. Don't feel so bad. Maybe you should lighten up." She chuck-led and nudged his arm.

He smiled. "You're cruel, Miss Lady. Really cruel. Here, let me walk you outside."

When they reached her car, he took her hand in his. "Thanks again for stopping by to check on me and bringing me soup and crackers and flowers."

"Of course," Katie said. She let go of his hand and climbed into the driver's seat.

In the rearview mirror, she could see Buck watching her drive off. Then he was out of sight as she rounded a curve.

Katie couldn't help but smile on her way home that evening as she thought about Buck. Pulling into the driveway of her house, she saw Matt and Randy sitting on the front porch.

"Uh-oh," she said as she stepped out of her car. "Should I be wor-ried? Am I in trouble?" She laughed.

"How is Buck?" Randy asked as she walked toward the front porch.

"He's feeling much better. I stopped and got him some soup, and he told me to tell you that he would be here in the morning."

Matt looked up at her and smiled. "No hello for me?"

"Hello, Matt." She squeezed his arm and went inside to fix a cup of coffee.

She came back out with her coffee and took a seat next to Matt. The three of them talked for a bit, then Randy stood up and grabbed his empty cup.

"Welp, I'm going to head on up and get ready for bed. Once you get to my age, the bed starts calling you earlier and earlier." Randy leaned over to hug Katie, shook Matt's hand, then headed in.

Katie rocked slowly in her chair and looked over at Matt. "So, how is Mr. Fuller this evening?"

"Not too shabby, Kat. I can't complain. But I did have a hard time sleeping last night. I couldn't stop thinking about that kiss that you and I shared."

"Yeah, it wrecked my brain, too, Matt," she said, and sighed. "It had been so long since I felt your breath on my face, your arms holding me. It's what I always wanted back then. I always dreamed of you coming back and us picking up where we left off."

"Me too. So, Katie ..." He turned to face her. "Do you think we can? I mean, I always thought you were okay waiting for me."

She glared at him. *Does he really think I was* okay *waiting on him all those years?* She needed to set him straight.

"Look, Matt, I was a shell when you left. And I did wait on you, but then you know what? I grew up. I quit putting my life on hold for a dream that I didn't ever think would happen again." She was surprised by her own abrasive tone, but in that moment, so many upsetting feelings were coming back.

"Kat, I-I'm sorry. I—"

"I think it would be best if we said goodnight, Matt." Tears were forming in her eyes. "It's been a long day." She stood up and went inside.

21

For several minutes, Matt sat there thinking about what had just happened. He'd never seen that side of Katie before, but he knew he didn't want to see it again. *Geez, Matt, why did you have to say that? You've really got to think before you open your mouth next time.*

But since Katie had gone inside, and he knew there was no way of making it right tonight, he set his empty glass next to his chair, stood up, and left.

CHAPTER FOUR

Joe's Place

Katie awoke the next day unsure of how to feel. She just wanted to be happy, or at least feel normal again, but instead, her emotions were all over the place.

"Ugh. Men always complicate the simple," she grumbled to herself as she slipped on a teal shirt—her most comfortable—along with a pair of light wash skinny jeans and light-brown cowgirl boots. She rounded out the look with burgundy lipstick, tied her hair up with a white bandana, and headed downstairs for some coffee.

Randy was already in the kitchen, and smiled at her when she walked in. "It's almost the big day, girl!"

Big day? she thought. *Oh my gosh, of course ... the fair!* In her frustration, Katie had forgotten all about it.

"Buck is on his way over," Randy said. "He called already to let me know he was feeling better."

She smiled. "My chicken noodle soup must've worked then."

"It sure did," Buck said, strolling into the kitchen.

"Buck! I didn't even hear you come in."

"Well, the door was open, and I—"

Her eyes lit up. "Buck, you shouldn't have!" She pointed at the bouquet of roses in his hand.

"Oh, yeah." Buck looked down at the roses, pulled out a card, and handed it to her. "I actually wish I would have," he said, "but I didn't. I assumed you left the door open because you were expecting me, but when I walked in, I saw these on the chair by the door. I'm guessing they're for you."

That's weird, she thought. *I don't remember the front door being open.* She must have forgotten to lock it last night after her angry exchange with Matt.

"Well?" Randy said. "What does the card say?"

Katie read the card to herself first, then out loud:

To my dearest Kat,

23

I never meant to hurt you with the words I said.
Please let me make it up to you. Dinner tonight? Our old spot.
Sincerely,
Matt

Their old spot was a little diner in town called Joe's Place. The owner, Joe Johnson, had the best food around for miles and made delicious pies. He had given Katie a few of his pie recipes and had even taken some time after close one evening to show her how to make them. After the fire at the farm, Joe brought home-cooked meals to Randy and Katie every week to help them out, something Katie would always be grateful for.

"Well, Randy, I'm gonna get to work," Buck said. "I have to make up for yesterday."

He walked past Katie, looked back at her, then walked out the back door. Katie put the flowers in a vase, carried them up to her room, and set them on the windowsill. She read the card again, then folded it and tapped it gently against her chin as she gazed out the window.

❧

Buck loaded hay onto the truck as fast as he could, trying to distract himself. He couldn't stop thinking about the kiss that had almost happened, and as a result, didn't sleep very well last night. That was bad enough. But walking in this morning to find roses some lover boy had left for *his* girl? It was like a hard slap in the face.

Buck tossed the last bale onto the truck and pulled the driver's-side door open. Before he could climb in, Randy walked up behind him.

"Wow," Randy said, giving a low, soft whistle. "I should really have Katie frustrate you more often, seeing how fast you loaded up all that hay."

"Yeah, well, it's all right. I'll get over it." Buck stepped up to get into the truck.

"Look, Buck," Randy said, placing his hand on Buck's arm. "It's obvious you care for her. I can see it in you just as I can see it in her."

Buck turned and looked down at Randy. *Is he saying Katie cares about me the way I care about her? Why didn't she ever say anything?*

And what's going on with this Matt guy, anyway? He hopped down onto the ground.

"You can see all that, Randy? How do you know?"

"I'm not blind," Randy said. "I can read Katie like a book, and I've been very close friends with you for years. I can tell from both of you. Now, look, she's going through a rough time right now, and what I need from you—what I am asking from you—is that you just be patient with her." Randy set his hand on Buck's shoulder. "Tomorrow, we'll go to the fair and have a great time. That's what she needs right now."

Buck mulled it over. Then he nodded, jumped in the truck, and sped off toward the barn.

After changing the sheets on all the beds upstairs and cleaning the bathrooms, Katie headed downstairs to start on the kitchen. Normally, Saturdays were her chore days, but she knew she'd want nothing to do with a bucket and mop tomorrow, the day of the fair.

Katie opened all the windows in the kitchen to let the fresh air in, then flicked on the radio above the countertop. One of her favorite songs was playing, and she couldn't help but hum along. As she mopped, she went from humming to singing, her hips seemingly moving on their own. She turned up the volume and sang even louder, boogeying from one side of the kitchen to the other. Then she spun around, grabbed the mop with one hand and twirled around it with the other, dancing her way past the window.

"Go, Katie!"

She stopped in her tracks, then backed up to peer out the kitchen window. There were Buck and her dad, dancing to the music, practically doubled over with laughter.

"You know you like it!" she yelled, giggling. She turned the music up and kept dancing.

In her bedroom later that day, Katie prepared to meet Matt at the diner. They had agreed on six o'clock, and it was already five. She didn't want to overdress, since it was just a diner, but at the same time, she didn't want to "bum it," as her mom would say. So she chose her favorite bur-

25

gundy tunic top and a pair of white skinny jeans to go with her knee-high, black boots. She put on her favorite white pearl pendant necklace, with earrings to match, along with a splash of lilac perfume, and out the door she went.

As she drove to the diner, Katie's head spun in circles with questions. *How much has Matt changed? Will I still enjoy his company? Will I still want to spend the rest of my life with him? And what about Buck?* She and Buck undoubtedly had a connection, and she couldn't deny her feelings for him.

Katie parked right under the tall, neon "Joe's Place" sign in the corner of the parking lot, like she always used to do. She stepped out of the car and looked over the diner for a few moments. It didn't seem like much had changed, at least from the outside.

The bell above the heavy door jingled as Katie pushed it open and walked in. She was greeted by the familiar smell of freshly baked pies and the sound of hamburgers sizzling.

Joe and one of his line cooks were both working the grill this evening. When Joe heard the bell, he looked up and did a double take. His mouth fell open, then turned into that wide, dimply grin she knew so well.

"Katie Calhoun!" Joe ran out from behind the counter and gave Katie a big hug. Tall and dashing with salt-and-pepper hair, dark-brown eyes, and broad shoulders, Joe had always reminded Katie of Danny Glover, the actor.

Joe stepped back and looked at her, beaming. "You are the last person I expected to see here tonight," he said. "It's so great to see you. How's your dad?"

"He's good, Joe," she said. "Everything is good. I'm sorry we haven't been here for a while."

"That's okay," he said. "What's important is that you're—"

The bell sounded and in walked Matt. Joe turned and his face lit up again.

"Well, I'll be! The surprises never cease," Joe said. "The old couple back together?" He grabbed two menus and pointed across the room. "Look at that, even your usual booth is open."

Their usual booth was in the corner of the restaurant, where they had a clear view of the movie theater just across the street. It was easy for them to see what was playing, so if they wanted to go to a movie after they ate, they would already know which one they wanted to see.

After Joe seated them, Katie turned her attention to Matt. He looked so handsome sitting there in front of her. His blue shirt matched his eyes, and he had left the top three buttons undone, which only made him look sexier. His scent brought her a feeling of comfort.

She quietly cleared her throat. "Matt, I apologize for last night. I was out of line," she said. "It's just that ... well, what you said rubbed me the wrong way."

"It's okay, Kat. What I said came out the wrong way. I meant that I knew how much we loved each other when I left that day, and I always thought there would be an 'us' when and if I were to come back. But I was selfish in thinking that you would always be here waiting for me." He reached his hand out across the table, and she took it.

"Look, Katie, I—"

The waitress appeared with their drinks and set them down on the table. She jotted down their food order and walked off.

"Look, Katie, I know you're going through a tough time, and you probably never expected to see me again. And now, there's another man who has your attention. I'm not saying you have to make a decision between him and me, I just want you to know that I never stopped loving you. I never stopped thinking about you. There is no other girl I found in California who was anywhere close to being you." He shrugged his shoulders and chuckled. "Trust me, I looked."

Katie smiled as a twinkle appeared in his eye. What he was saying was sweet. For a moment, she felt sad that she had started having feelings for Buck, but she stopped herself. She liked Buck, too. Besides, if she and Matt got together, he would want her to move to California, and she couldn't do that. She didn't want to do that. Her life was here, in Orange Grove, Georgia.

Their burgers arrived. As they ate, they talked of old times, mostly their high school days. Then Katie asked about his job in California, and he told her he had found work as an accountant.

"So, I have these wealthy clients," he said, "and I get paid good money to do their taxes. And ... let's just say ... sweep things under the rug. Not really something I'm proud of, but hey, money talks, you know?"

"Of course," Katie said. "But ..." She thought about how to phrase her question. "Doesn't that bother you, though? Having to basically lie all the time?"

He took a long sip of soda through his straw, then shrugged. "It did at first," he said. "But honestly, it's not a ton of money. And plus, the IRS has so many bigger things they need to deal with."

Soon after they finished their meal, the waitress dropped off their check, which Matt took care of. Katie gave Joe another hug before they left and promised not to stay away too long. She also promised to bring her dad next time.

"By the way, I want an invite to the wedding!" Joe yelled as they walked out the door. That made Katie giggle.

Because it was such a pleasant evening, they decided to leave their cars at the diner and go for a walk. They strolled past the movie theater, down the block to the ice cream parlor, then through the park, reminiscing the whole time about their memories together. On the way back, they stopped at the concrete fountain in front of the courthouse. Aqua-colored floodlights lit up the water, giving it a mysterious, blue glow. Katie sat down on the circular edge of the fountain, mesmerized by all the coins shimmering at the bottom.

"Remember when we used to do this, Katie?" Matt said, reaching into his pocket.

Katie smiled. "I sure do."

"Here, take some coins. Now, close your eyes and make a wish," Matt said. He placed his hand on her shoulder.

She looked up at him, then at the water. She closed her eyes, took a deep breath, and tossed her coins into the fountain. When she opened her eyes, Matt was sitting right next to her. His eyes were almost the same color as the water. He leaned in to kiss her as he brought his other leg up and over the low concrete wall. He put his hand down to steady himself, and as he did, Katie shifted her position slightly, causing Matt to lose his grip and ... *splash!* He fell into the water.

Katie gasped and put her hand to her mouth. "Oh my gosh, Matt!" She stood and balanced herself on the edge to try and help him, but by the time she reached her hand out, he was already standing, the water from the fountain plopping onto his head.

He cracked a smile, and she burst out laughing. "Matt," she said, "you're supposed to throw your change in, not yourself! That must have been some wish!"

A gush of water splashed out from the bottom of his shirt as he untucked it from his pants and trudged out of the fountain. He looked more serious now, and she had to stifle her laughter. Matt stood in front of Katie and looked deep into her eyes. A drop of water ran down his face.

"I'm due to be leaving on Wednesday, Kat," he said. "I have a meeting with a client, and I can't miss it." He took her hands into his. They were freezing. Now she felt bad for laughing at his misfortune, but she reminded herself that he'd laughed, too.

"Come with me, Kat," he said. "To California. You can see my folks again, see where I live, where I work. I can give you the grand tour."

She stared at him, not sure what to think.

"Wha ... what about my dad?" she said. "What about everything I need to do here?"

She let go of his hands and slowly walked away from him, taking in what he was saying.

He walked after her, his waterlogged shoes squishing with every step. "I think he can manage for a couple of days, Kat. Plus, Buck could stay with him while you're away." He sounded excited, like he had the whole thing planned out. "Think of it as a vacation. It might be nice for you to get away for a bit." He took her hands in his again.

Maybe he was right, she thought. A few days in California could be just what she needed. The beaches, the sand, the sunsets—it really did sound like paradise to her.

"Let me talk to my dad about it first, Matt," she said, looking into his eyes. "I'll let you know."

As they walked back to the diner, Matt told Katie that he would be looking at a few houses with his friend over the weekend, and that he probably wouldn't see her until Monday.

"That's fine," she said, brushing a few stray curls out of her face. "I'm sorry you won't be able to come to the fair, though."

"I'm sorry, too," he said. "If anything changes, I'll let you know." They hugged and he opened her car door for her. As she turned out of the parking lot, she saw Matt in her side mirror, watching her drive off.

When she got home, she sat her purse down on the chair by the front door and walked into the kitchen. It was still as clean as she had left it, even though it smelled of fried chicken and mashed potatoes and gravy. *Dad probably had Bo's for dinner*, she thought. Bo's was a takeout joint in town that they'd order from whenever none of them felt like cooking. The lingering aroma brought back pleasant memories of many a family meal growing up.

She opened the fridge and pulled out her pitcher of iced tea just as Randy walked in.

"How did it go, Katie? All forgiven?" He sat down at the table as she poured herself a glass of tea.

"Yeah, Dad. All is forgiven." She took a sip. "Dad, can I talk to you?"

"Of course, Peach. You can tell me anything." He patted her hands as she sat down to face him.

"Matt wants me to go back with him to California for a few days, and I don't know if I want to go. I mean, I would like to, but ..."

"When does he want you to go with him?"

She leaned back in her chair. "Well, he's going with his friend to see some houses this weekend, so he won't be leaving until Wednesday," she said, staring at the floor. "The thing is, I just don't want to leave you and everything here for all that time."

"Look, Katie, I'm a big boy," he said. "Sure, I'll miss you, but we're talking, what, two or three days? Besides, I'm sure Buck wouldn't mind spending a few days here."

"That's exactly what Matt said." Katie smiled and stood up.

"Why don't you get some rest," Randy said. He smiled at her. "Sleep on it and give yourself time to think it over. Tomorrow is the fair!"

"You're right," she said, hugging her father goodnight. "You're the greatest, Daddy. Thanks."

She walked out of the kitchen and made her way upstairs for the night.

CHAPTER FIVE

The Fair

The next morning, Katie noticed it as soon as she walked into her bedroom: a cup of coffee, still steaming, sitting on her dresser. She loved how her daddy spoiled her. He must have put it there just before she finished her shower. Hints of hazelnut and mocha embraced her as she took a sip. He had made her favorite.

Looking out the window, Katie would have sworn the sun was shining more brightly than usual over the mountaintops. "It really will be a great day!" she said to herself as she rummaged through her closet to find an outfit for the fair. She picked out a summer dress with blue and white flowers and slipped on her white wedge sandals.

As she sat down at her dresser to put on makeup, she looked down at the picture of her mother that was taped to the bottom of the mirror. If her mom were here with them now, she'd be so excited for Katie. Just knowing that made Katie feel even more hopeful. She finished her makeup, pulled her hair back into a ponytail, and headed downstairs.

Randy stood in front of the stove, stirring eggs in a pan. He turned around and smiled when Katie walked in. "Well, don't you look like a petal on a daisy, Peach!"

"Aww. Thanks, Daddy." Katie sat down at the table. "Have you heard anything from Buck yet?"

"He called me a little while ago. He'll probably be here within the hour."

From her seat, Katie could see out the French doors that led to the back, and she gazed into the vast fields of green. Suddenly she was in one of those fields, at dusk, dancing with Buck under the rising moon. He held her close to his body as they moved in perfect rhythm with each other. She buried her face in his muscular chest, the smell of his cologne driving her wild. She looked up at him, stared into his eyes, and prepared her lips for a kiss. He lowered his face to hers.

"Katie?" her father said, waving the hot pan of eggs near her plate. "I said, are you hungry?"

"Oh, yeah. I'm sorry." She shook her head.

Randy laughed. "You sure were lost in that daydream." He scooped a helping of eggs onto Katie's plate.

She laughed, too, because she really couldn't argue. "I'm just so torn on what to do, Daddy. I can dream all day, and sometimes all night, about each of them, and when I'm alone with either one, it just feels right."

"Matters of the heart are the hardest to deal with, Peach," he said, casting a glance at her plate. "Well, I'll let you eat before your food gets cold. What is it you're always telling me about breakfast?"

"It's the most important meal of the day, of course," she said, smiling. She felt better already.

᎐

Buck hopped into his car, excited to see Katie and spend the day with her at the fair. On the way over, he stopped at Merriman's Fresh Market to pick up a surprise for Katie.

"Good morning, Buck," Frank Merriman said with a smile. "Can I help you with anything?"

"No, I don't reckon so, Frank," he said. "Katie and I are going to the fair today, and there's one thing that I know will brighten up her day." He kept walking and headed straight for the flowers.

From behind the floral counter, Violet smiled and greeted him with a look of surprise on her face. "I don't think I've ever seen you stopping to buy flowers here, Buck," she said. "What's the occasion?"

"Well, Katie and I are going to the fair today, and I ..." He must have passed the flower display a hundred times but was only now noticing how eye-popping all the colors were. The arrangements were gorgeous, and the flowers looked as fresh as if they'd just been picked out of a garden ...

"I'm sorry, I got distracted by how beautiful all these flowers are," he said. "I'm looking for some daisies for Katie."

Violet pointed out the daisies and he carefully chose the ones he liked best. Then she arranged the flowers and tied a purple ribbon around them.

"You sure have good taste," she said, handing him the bouquet.

He tipped his hat and smiled. "Thank you, ma'am."

"Wow," Frank said as Buck walked up to the checkout counter. "Violet sure did them up pretty, didn't she?"

"She sure did," Buck said as he handed him cash to pay for the flowers. "Katie will love them. Daisies are her all-time favorite."

Frank counted back Buck's change. "Y'all have a great time today," he said. Buck thanked him and said goodbye.

Arriving at the house, Buck rang the doorbell and hid the flowers behind his back. While he waited, he checked out his reflection in the window of the door: dark-wash jeans, black cowboy boots, loose-fitting white shirt, and black Stetson. He knew he looked good, but there was only one person he was hoping to impress today. He gave his hat a last-minute adjustment.

Randy opened the door. "My, my, we're all dressed up fancy for today, aren't we?" he said. "Come on in. Katie's in the living room."

Buck thought Randy looked dapper himself, sporting a pair of blue jeans, navy polo pullover, and his new, black-and-silver bolo tie. As they walked into the living room, Katie jumped up and ran over to give Buck a hug. He pulled the flowers out from behind his back and handed them to Katie.

"William Buck Brady, these are the most beautiful flowers. They're amazing," she said. "Aww, you know how much I love daisies!"

She left to put the flowers in a vase, then came back and set them in the front window. "That way," she said, "when the sun hits them every morning, it will make them even more beautiful."

"All right," Randy said, clasping his hands together. "If you're both ready to hit the road, we've got a fair to go to."

Katie was in the car before either of them had made it out of the house. She felt like a child on Christmas morning, about to tear into all the presents under the tree. Buck and her dad looked at each other and laughed when they came out and saw her sitting in the car.

The fair was set up on a large, grassy field about ten miles out of town. As they approached, Katie could see the bright-white Ferris wheel turning from a distance. Even from here, it was so much bigger than she remembered.

The main parking lots were all full, so an attendant directed Randy to an overflow lot. "I hope your feet don't get too tired from walking around," Randy said as they got out of the car. "It'll be a hike getting back here later tonight."

Katie didn't care. She was ready to sprint to the fairgrounds and jump on every single ride.

"Last one to the Ferris wheel is a rotten egg!" she yelled and tore off. Buck ran after her.

"I guess I'll be rotten, y'all," Randy called out, chuckling. "You two go on ahead."

"I'll get you, my pretty," Buck yelled from behind her, holding up his hands and cackling like a witch.

Katie squealed and ran even faster. When they reached the Ferris wheel, Katie insisted she had won fair and square.

"You're the rotten egg," Katie said, out of breath.

Buck tipped his hat and conceded. They sat down on a bench and caught their breath. A few minutes later, Randy walked up.

"I see you still have your running feet, Peach," he said. He looked over at Buck. "She's fast, ain't she?"

"Wait, you knew she could run like that and didn't tell me?"

"I sure did," Randy said, smiling. "She was winning left and right when she was on the high school track team."

"Why, you little ..." Buck reached out and gave her a playful squeeze.

Katie could wait no longer. "Come on!" She grabbed Buck's hands and pulled him off the bench. "Let's go ride some rides!"

"You guys go have some fun," Randy said. "I'm gonna head over here and look at these old cars. Just give me a call when you're finished."

They scurried off and made a beeline for the Swing-o-Matic: a ride with swings suspended by long chains that would lift them high off the ground and spin them in circles. Katie couldn't wait.

When it was their turn, Katie climbed into the swing right beside Buck and hooked the safety strap across her lap. She looked over at Buck, who was staring straight ahead, squeezing the chains.

"What's wrong, Buck?"

"Huh? Nothing, I just ... I mean, seeing all those people swinging way up there—"

"Wait, you're not ..." Katie said as a smile spread across her face. "Are you telling me a big, strong man like yourself is afraid of heights?" She reached her foot out and gave his swing a sideways push.

34

Buck tightened his grip. "No ma'am," he said. "I'm not afraid of heights so much as I'm afraid of falling."

With a loud clank, the ride started up. They looked at each other, and Buck gave Katie a wan smile. All the color had drained from his face. As their swings rose into the air and picked up speed, Katie held her arms out by her sides as if she were a bird soaring across the sky. The wind in her hair made her feel free. Buck, on the other hand, kept his iron grip on the chains the whole time.

Once they were back on the ground, Katie teased him. "I guess I won't make you ride any of the rides that go up that high anymore." She giggled.

Buck held his stomach. "Yes, or any of them that go around in circles like that. My goal is to eat all the delicious food here, not give it all back."

They laughed as they walked on. He was so funny. And she was amazed at what a good sport he was, even joining her on a ride he knew he wouldn't enjoy.

"Speaking of food," Katie said as they came across a line of food carts, "are you hungry?"

"After that last ride, I'm not so sure," he said, looking at all the carts. "But I could probably go for something sweet."

"Ooooo, that one! I want to try that one," Katie exclaimed, pointing to the sign that had caught her eye:

FRIED COOKIE DOUGH

NOT

YOUR

MOMMA'S

COOKIE

Katie's mouth watered as the food cart employee drizzled chocolate sauce over the plate of still-steaming fried dough balls and handed it to her. As she carefully bit into one, she held the plate out for Buck to help himself.

She threw Buck a big smile, and he burst out laughing. "That's the chocolatiest grin I've ever seen," he said. "Here, I'll get us some cold milk to go along with this." He ordered a small bottle of milk for them to share, then popped one of the dough balls into his mouth. She laughed when she saw he had chocolate on his teeth, too. They were like a couple of two-year-olds making a gooey, chocolatey mess.

Just as they had eaten the last of the fried cookie dough and finished off the milk, Randy walked up carrying his own fair food find. In his hands was the biggest, most extravagant hot dog Katie had ever seen: a whole foot long and smothered in relish, onions, chili, and cheese, with healthy dollops of ketchup and mustard on top.

"Oh my goodness, Dad!" Katie said. "What the heck is that?"

"It's the King Coney," he said, beaming. "I love these, but it's not every day I get to have one. Plus, I'm not riding any rides, so I don't have to worry about it coming back up."

He took a bite, then looked up at the sky and mouthed the words "thank you."

By dusk, Katie and Buck had been on every attraction at the fair except for one: the Gravitron. Even though Buck had vowed not to go on any rides that spun him in circles, Katie really wanted to try it, and begged him to come along.

He finally agreed, and the Gravitron spun him literally sick. Katie found a bench for them to sit down on while she rubbed his back and held a wet paper towel to his forehead.

She smiled at him. "I'm so sorry, Buck. I guess we should've stopped when I noticed your balance was wobbly."

"Well, it's not like you twisted my arm to get on that thing. I could've said no." Buck looked over at her and smiled weakly.

Just then, a slow, pretty song started playing somewhere across the fairgrounds. "What do you say we walk it off and head toward the music, Buck?" Katie said as she rubbed the side of his face. She was in the mood to dance.

Standing and gaining not only his balance but also his composure, he accepted her invitation.

CHAPTER SIX

Fireworks and Secrets

The music led them over to the Ferris wheel, where a large trellis had been set up for dancing. Strands of white lights that twinkled between white and purple flowers were wrapped around each post. Draped across the lattice ceiling were strings of Mason jars, each with a tiny light inside. For Katie, the decorations were perfect. Simple yet beautiful. Clearly, the fair staff had put time and effort into making this an evening to remember.

Katie looked around to see where her father had gotten off to and spotted him sitting at one of the nearby wooden picnic tables. She waved to him and motioned toward the trellis to show him how beautiful it was. He gave her a big smile and thumbs up. When she turned back around, Buck was standing in front of her, holding out his hand for her to take. She was mesmerized by his tan skin against the white of his shirt, his jet-black hair neatly tucked under his cowboy hat, the glow of the glass jars behind him.

He bent forward slightly. "May I have this dance, fair maiden?"

Katie almost giggled at his humorous, overly formal request, but the moment was too romantic to laugh. Like Prince Charming, he made her feel like a princess. All she wanted was to melt into his arms.

"You may, sir." She curtsied.

He led her under the trellis where several other couples were already swaying to the music. The slow song did nothing to calm her racing heart as he pulled her in close and wrapped his arms around her waist. The scent of his cologne surrounded her and brought her a feeling of comfort. How easy it would be to fall in love with him, she thought. Then: *Have I already?*

"Katie," Buck whispered.

"Yes, Buck?" She looked up and gazed into his eyes.

"Do you really have to go with Matt to California next week?"

The question caught her off guard. *How did he know about that?* she wondered, before realizing her dad must have told him. But the situation with Matt was the last thing she was thinking about right now—and for that matter, the last thing she wanted to think about.

37

"Well, it would be nice to see his parents and see how he's been doing there," she said. "And you know how much I love the beach."

"Do I?" Buck said. "Well, as long as the only thing you fall in love with there is the ocean, I guess it'll be okay." He returned her gaze and held her closer as the song came to an end. They stepped out of the trellis and walked toward the picnic tables.

Randy looked up and saw them approaching. "Hey, you guys. Are you hungry?" he said.

Katie's eyes grew wide. "You mean to tell me you're hungry again after that giant-sized hot dog you ate?"

"Oh no, not me," Randy said, rubbing his tummy. "I don't think I'll eat for the rest of the week."

They all laughed. Just then, a deep voice blared from the loud-speakers and echoed throughout the fairgrounds: "It's that time of night, folks ... fireworks time! Keep your eyes on the skies. That's right, keep your eyes on the skies because the show's starting soooooon!"

"Come on, guys, come on!" Katie said.

They hurried over to the other side of the Ferris wheel to get a clear view of the fireworks. Katie stared up at the pitch-black sky, waiting for it to light up. *If only Mom were here,* she thought. *She was always excited about fireworks. She'd be beside herself right now.*

BOOM! The first firework sailed up into the sky. Katie had forgotten how loud they were, but that didn't deter her from standing there. She cheered for more as a shower of red, green, and blue lit up the fairgrounds.

Buck walked up behind her and wrapped his arms around her waist. She sighed and leaned back against him, staring skyward to watch each colorful explosion. Katie had to cover her ears during the grand finale, but it was a fitting end to a perfect night.

They hopped in the car to go back home around ten o'clock. Katie dozed off in the back seat as her dad went on and on about how delicious that hot dog was. When they arrived home, they all sat out on the porch. The night was quiet, and a light breeze tickled the seashell wind chime every now and again to break the silence. Katie stretched and yawned.

"Someone ready for bed?" Randy said, looking over at her.

"Yeah, you're right about that, Daddy. I'm pooped."

"Me too," Randy said, standing up. "I'm going to bid you both goodnight and see about getting some shuteye." He shook Buck's hand, kissed the top of Katie's head, and walked toward the front door.

Buck also yawned and rubbed his eyes. "I'm not too far behind you guys. I'd better get home while I can still drive." He chuckled.

Katie and Buck said their goodnights and hugged. As they stepped away from one another, Buck gently lifted Katie's chin so he could look directly into her eyes.

"Katie," Buck said, "I can't hide how I feel for you anymore. I have loved you since I first saw you, but I also respect you and your feelings. I won't push mine on you when you're not ready or sure you feel the same for me. I know that you and Matt have a past, and I know that you need to sort that out. But I want you to know that I will wait for you until you're ready. If you decide you should be with Matt, I will understand and will always be a friend to you. If you pick me, I will always be there for you no matter what. I will ensure that your every need is met and that you want for nothing. I had the greatest time with you today, darlin'."

Katie's mind spun. That was a lot to take in, and she didn't know quite what to think or say.

Instead, she leaned back and giggled. "You mean you even had a great time on the Gravitron?"

"Even the Gravitron, Katie. Maybe not what happened right after that, but everything before." He laughed.

"You want to know what I liked, Buck?"

He smiled. "What was your favorite part of the day, Katie?"

"Dancing," she said, leaning in toward him. "With you."

He lowered his face to meet hers, and she stood a little taller to meet his. Their lips were practically touching.

Finally, she thought. *I get to taste those sweet lips, the ones I've wanted for so long.*

Crack! Katie whipped around. It sounded like a branch had been snapped in half somewhere in the wooded area behind them.

She looked back at Buck. "What was that?"

"I don't know." His eyes darted back and forth.

Katie walked slowly toward the trees that started just past the porch. "Hello?" she called out. "Is someone there?"

Buck grabbed her shoulder. "It could be anything, Katie. You may not want to venture too close."

He ran over to his truck and came back with a flashlight and a pistol. He walked the tree line and shined the flashlight in as far as he could. The woods were too thick to enter, but he swept the light across the area until he was sure there wasn't anything or anyone there.

"Maybe we should get my dad," Katie said.

"Let your dad get some sleep," he said. "You should get some sleep as well. I'll keep watch for a little while before I leave, and I promise if I see anything, I'll call for you." Buck rubbed her arms. "Go inside, darlin'."

Katie reluctantly agreed, kissed his cheek, and went into the house.

The next morning, Katie woke up to the smell of eggs and bacon. The sun was already streaming through her window. She'd slept later than usual. She slipped her silky robe over her blue-plaid pajamas and went downstairs to greet the day.

"Good morning!" Randy said as Katie padded into the kitchen. He handed her a fresh cup of coffee.

"Thanks, Daddy. This is such a treat." She took several quick sips of her coffee. She needed to wake up. "We had a little scare outside last night after you went to bed."

"What?" His eyes widened. "What scare? What happened?"

"I was saying goodbye to Buck last night, and we heard a loud noise in the woods behind us, almost like a really big animal was back there, or even a person. Buck had a flashlight, and he looked around in the trees but didn't see anything. Then I went to bed, and he said he would stick around for a while to make sure it was safe before he went home."

"I can't believe it, Peach. I went right to bed after my shower last night. I must have slept through—"

The phone on the wall rang. Randy walked over and picked it up.

"Hello?" he said. "Yes, this is he. Who is this, please?"

All Katie could hear was a deep, gruff voice on the other line. She shot her dad a questioning look.

"Actually, my daughter was just telling me about something that happened last night, probably around ten o'clock. As far as I know, everything is—yes, that would be fine. What time? Sure, see you then." Randy hung up.

"What was all that about, Dad?"

Randy sat down and stared straight ahead. "It was the police. His name was Sergeant Haskins. Apparently, there were other disturbances in the area last night, too. He'll be stopping by the farm a little later." He looked over at Katie. "Well, now I'm a little worried, Peach."

The front door opened, and Randy jumped. Before Katie could get up to look, Buck strolled into the kitchen.

"Whew, Buck, you scared us," Katie said, sighing with relief.

"I'm sorry," Buck said. "I shouldn't have let myself in like that, but I just wanted to check on you guys. After last night, I couldn't sleep.

40

I know I'm probably overreacting. It was just one little noise, and it could have been anything." He looked over at Randy. "Wait, does your dad know about—"

"Yes, I told him," Katie said. "In fact, we just got a call from the police about it."

"They're coming by this afternoon to look around," Randy said. "They had other disturbance reports, and they want to see if the incidents might be connected."

Katie got up and poured two glasses of sweet tea with ice. She handed one to Buck.

"Well, whether it was just a raccoon, or a large dog, or something more," Buck said, taking a sip of his tea, "I just want to be here to make sure nothing happens to you guys."

"Show me where you heard the noise from," Randy said, and the three of them walked out to the front porch.

"We were standing right here," Buck said, "and I was just getting ready to give Katie a hug and leave, and we heard a loud snap. Almost like something or someone was over there." Buck pointed to the trees behind them. "We looked, but we couldn't see anybody."

Randy sighed. "Those trees are so thick that it would be hard to see anyone in there." He shook his head. "This is my fault, you guys. I should have had this whole area thinned out like I had planned years ago."

"Don't blame yourself, Daddy," Katie said. "We don't know anything yet. Let's just let the police take care of it when they get here. Their job is to investigate things."

At two o'clock, a black SUV with tinted windows pulled up in front of the house. Randy walked outside and was approaching the vehicle when a uniformed officer stepped out.

"I'm Sergeant Haskins," he said, extending his hand. "You must be Randy. We've got a few more units on their way. I just want to assure you that we will be handling this and making sure every inch of your property is searched. I know it's an inconvenience, sir, and I know it can be scary, but I don't want you to worry about a thing."

CHAPTER SEVEN

California Dreaming

As Matt Fuller drove up to the farm, he saw the black SUV and several other police vehicles parked on the driveway. *What on Earth?* Pulling into the bottom part of the driveway, he hit the brakes, stirring up a cloud of dust. He put the car in park and jumped out. Some of the officers were standing on the driveway, others were prowling about in the trees along the side of the house.

He spotted Randy, Katie, and Buck on the porch and ran toward them. "What's going on here?" he yelled.

Randy stepped off the porch to meet him. "Hey, Matt, it's okay. Good to see you. Everything's okay."

"But what is all of this?" He looked over at Katie as he tried to catch his breath. "My goodness, Kat, are you okay? I don't see you for two days, and now there are police all over your property? What's going on?"

Katie came over and wrapped her arms around him in a tight bear hug. When they were younger, Katie would always be the one to bring him comfort in times of panic. That was one of her concerns when she found out he would be moving to California: who would be there to calm him down?

"Matt, take a deep breath and come over here," Katie said. "I'll try to explain what's going on, or at least what I know so far." Matt sat down on one of the porch chairs while Katie told him about the noise they'd heard and the call they'd received from the police sergeant that morning.

"I'm just glad y'all are okay," Matt said. He seemed to have calmed down a bit.

"I'm sure it's nothing," Katie said. "These guys are just doing their job in making sure we're all safe. We just need to keep our guard up and stay vigilant."

"Well, I came over to see if you were still planning to join me when I go back to California," Matt said.

"I don't know if that's such a good idea now, Matt," Katie said, looking around at the officers scouring the woods. "As you can see, there's a lot going on here, and I wouldn't feel comfortable leaving my dad."

43

"I can understand that, Katie, but can't Buck stay over here and watch out for him?"

Katie knew Buck could handle that assignment. She also knew that her dad could handle being under Buck's twenty-four-seven watch. But what she didn't know was whether she could handle being so far away with all that going on.

Katie thought it over. "Tell you what," she said. "Today is Sunday. If nothing comes of this search by—"

"Sergeant!" one of the officers yelled as he emerged from the wooded area. Sergeant Haskins and two other officers ran over to meet him.

"I found a piece of black string and some footprints back there, sir," the officer said. He showed Sergeant Haskins the photos he had taken.

"All right, let's get some evidence bags and start combing that area for more clues," Sergeant Haskins told his team. He looked at Randy. "So, none of you ever go into these woods?"

"No, sir. It's much too overgrown," Randy said, then chuckled and patted his stomach. "I couldn't fit back there if I tried."

Sergeant Haskins pulled a small pad of paper out of his pocket and walked along the tree line, making notes as he looked around. A few minutes later, he came back to Randy.

"Well, this is what we have so far," he said. "The footprints were pointing toward your house, and the brush was matted down. This tells me someone was standing there for quite some time, not just walking through. The black string was found behind the footprints, which indicates whoever it was had a bag of some sort. Or it could've been thread from their clothing. Either way, I would say there's a good chance you guys have someone watching you."

"Watching us?" Katie asked. "Why would anyone want to watch us?"

The sergeant tapped the end of his pen on his notepad. "From the spot with the footprints, a person would have a clear view of the whole front porch and the upstairs window on the side of the house. Does that window go to an attic or something?"

"No, Sergeant Haskins." Her head spun. "That window goes to my room!"

Katie had to sit down. She always changed clothes near that window. Was whoever this was watching her change? She left the window cracked in the summertime to let fresh air in. Did this sicko hear her humming as she read her favorite book? Watch her as she lay in bed before she fell asleep? What about all the times she sat on the porch at night to watch the sunset in her favorite rocking chair, thinking she was alone? Was she being watched then and just didn't know it? She felt sick to her stomach.

Randy sat down and put his arm around her. "We'll take care of this, Peach. Don't worry."

He looked at Sergeant Haskins, who was flipping through his notepad. "Sergeant, does this in any way seem connected to the other disturbances in the area?"

"It may all be tied together, or it may be separate occurrences," he said. "We don't have enough evidence to go on right now. As soon as I know something, y'all will know something."

Matt shook his head. "That's not good enough. Kat shouldn't stay here, so I'll tell you what's going to happen. Kat's coming to California with me. And guess what? Forget Wednesday. We'll be leaving today."

Buck glowered at him. "Now, let's not get crazy. We don't even know the full story yet. Plus, I don't think Katie would feel comfortable leaving her dad right now."

"Well, she sure as hell ain't gonna feel comfortable sleeping in her room after—"

"Guys!" Katie said. They both looked over at her. "Chill out, you two. I'll be fine. I know they'll catch whoever this is. And I'm not going anywhere with anyone today. That is, unless ..." She looked at all of them. "Unless you guys want to go to the fair? Take our minds off all this?"

"That's a great idea," Randy said. "Let's all head over there."

"If it's all right with you," Sergeant Haskins said, "me and my guys will stay here and look for more evidence."

"Fine by me. If you need to reach me, I'll have my cell phone."

Katie hopped in the car with her dad, leaving Matt and Buck to drive together, and they set off for the fair. The change of scenery, along with knowing the police were on the case, made Katie feel a little better. She just wanted some reassurance that things were not as crazy as they seemed and would be okay in the end.

She looked back at the car Matt and Buck were in, wondering how they were getting along. She hoped they could form at least a little bit of a friendship. What she surely didn't need was the two of them bickering. There was too much going on for that.

When they got to the fair, they all sat down at a picnic table that faced the Ferris wheel. Randy walked off and came back with a round of lemonades for the group.

As she sipped her drink, Katie lost herself in the atmosphere of the fair. Squeals of laughter as kids darted off to their favorite rides, the loud clacking of metal as the roller coaster swept by, the smell of fair food. It all helped her relax. She took a long sip of lemonade and tried to decide what to do about the situation at home.

Knowing there wasn't much she could do at that moment, she set her cup down, grabbed Buck's hand, and pulled him up.

"Last one to the Zipper is a rotten egg!" She let go of Buck's hand and ran off.

∽

Randy chuckled as Katie bolted away, but Matt wasn't amused. *Why did she choose Buck just now?* Maybe she knew he wasn't much for fair rides, but still, he wanted her to desire his company like she used to. And now she'd fallen for some pretty boy farmhand who was always coming on to her. Matt tapped his car keys on the table as he watched people milling about the fairgrounds.

Randy glanced in his direction. "What's wrong, Matt?"

Matt looked over at Randy and took a sip of his lemonade.

"I'm just worried about Katie," he said. "I asked her if she would come to California with me, and she said she would. But now that she has someone stalking her, she thinks it's better to stay here. I just want to make sure she's safe."

"Matt, don't you think we want the same thing for her?" Randy said. "Do you think we want her to be the victim of some stalker or prowler or whatever this person is? Look, that girl is my life, and she means a lot to a lot of people. We're going to do everything in our power to keep her safe."

"I know, sir." Matt finished his lemonade and took a long, deep breath. "I know that as her dad, you will do it with all your might. It's just … I love her."

Katie and Buck came running back and sat down at the table. Matt was glad to see her in good spirits, but wished it was because of him, not that other guy.

"So," Randy said, "who was the rotten egg?"

Buck smiled. "Who do you think?"

"It was me," Katie said, patting him on the back. "It turns out he was just letting me win all those times. He decided that if I was going to force him to go on the Zipper, he would at least make me the rotten egg."

"Finally," Randy said, "I see my little girl has some running competition."

✧

Just before nightfall, Randy's cell phone rang. It was Sergeant Haskins telling him they were all packed up and leaving for the day. He said they'd gathered more evidence at the house and would be in touch once they'd examined it.

"Well, Peach," Randy said after telling her the news, "what would you like to do now?"

Katie didn't want to go home. She still wasn't ready and didn't know if she'd ever feel comfortable in her room again knowing someone could be watching her. Would she be forced to keep her window closed and curtains drawn forever? She loved waking up to the sun shining through her window, but now she wouldn't feel safe leaving her curtains open.

She looked at Matt and Buck and sighed. "What do you guys want to do?"

"Bowling?" Buck said. "You know I'm always up for a good game." He made the motion of rolling a ball toward the pins.

That struck her as hilarious, and she laughed harder than she meant to.

"I know," Randy said. "Let's go to Joe's!"

"Daddy, that's a great idea! Joe made me promise to bring you next time I went."

Buck and Matt headed for the parking lot while Katie fell back with Randy. She reached out her hand for his as they walked.

Randy looked over at her. "Been a long while since you've held hands with your dear old dad, Katie. Are you all right?"

"What?" Katie said, smiling at him. "I can't hold hands with my dad for no reason?"

He laughed. "No, that's not at all what I'm saying."

He was right. It had been a while. But holding her dad's hand made her feel safer and more at ease.

47

"There's a lot going on, and I'm just so thankful that you're here for me and with me, Dad." She looked at him and smiled.

"Of course, Peach. Where else would I be?"

There were only a handful of cars in the parking lot of the diner, and through the windows she could see that half the tables were empty. It didn't surprise Katie that with the fair in town, it would be a slow Sunday night.

The bell jingled as Randy pushed the heavy door open. "Have a seat, folks, and we'll be with you in a moment," Joe called out from the grill without looking up.

"But what if I want *you* to seat me?" Randy called back, smiling.

Joe looked up and his eyes widened. "Randy Calhoun!" His trademark grin spread across his face.

He came out from behind the counter and gave him a big hug. Smiling, he looked at Katie, then Matt, then Buck.

"My goodness," he said. "It's all y'all!"

Randy laughed. "Well, we were just at the fair and worked up quite the appetite. We couldn't think of anywhere else we'd rather eat."

"Oh, you're funning me!" Joe laughed and gave a dismissive wave of his hand. "I'm by myself at the grill tonight so I have to get back, but we'll get y'all seated right away."

CHAPTER EIGHT

Cloudy with a Side of Bacon

Eating at Joe's was always a great idea. Laughing and sharing stories of old times with the most important people in her life was the perfect backdrop for a delicious meal of burgers, fries, and milkshakes. It took Katie's mind off everything and helped her almost forget about the situation back at the farm.

She looked around. The other patrons had left long ago, and Joe was wiping down the counter.

Randy spoke up. "Well, I'm sure Joe wants to close up shop soon. Why don't we get out of here so he can do what he needs to do."

Joe walked over to the table. "For a minute there, I thought you guys might be spending the night." He laughed.

Randy cleared his throat. "Yeah, sorry about that, Joe."

"Please, I was kidding," Joe said, placing one hand on Randy's shoulder and giving his upper arm a squeeze with the other. It's no problem at all. It was nice to have you guys all in here." They said goodbye to Joe and piled back into their cars to return to the farm.

Randy pulled the car into the driveway, and Matt parked right behind him. With the headlights illuminating the front of the house, images of officers searching the property flashed before Katie's eyes. She suddenly wished she were back at the fair so she could forget about it.

Matt got out of the car and tapped on Randy's window. "We're going to take a look around before you get out," he said. "Why don't you two stay in the car until we give you the all-clear."

For the next fifteen minutes, Matt and Buck searched the premises with flashlights, peering as far into the trees as they could. Buck forced his way through to the area where the first pieces of evidence were found.

"This just seems so surreal, Daddy," Katie said, watching Matt and Buck look around. "It's like one of those mystery shows on TV, except I wish someone would jump out of the woods and tell me they were just kidding. Tell me they were just filming a TV show, and it was all a joke."

Randy chuckled. "Those poor guys would fall over if anyone jumped out of the woods right now!"

49

Katie laughed at the idea. "That's true, Dad. Almost worth seeing if it weren't such a serious situation."

Matt and Buck walked back to the car, and Randy rolled down his window. "It's all clear," Matt said. "You're safe to go in. We didn't see anything." He walked around to Katie's side and opened her door.

"Maybe whoever this was saw the police here earlier and got scared," Buck said.

"We really appreciate you guys doing this for us," Randy said, shaking their hands. "By the way, Joe is heading down to the farmers' market tomorrow morning and invited us to go with him. Why don't you two meet us here around nine-thirty for breakfast and we'll head to the market together?"

"Sounds good to me," Buck said.

"I'll have to decline, sir," Matt said. "I have to start getting my stuff together for the trip home." He gave Katie a hug. "Be safe, Kat," he said, resting his chin on her shoulder. "If you need anything, you call me right away." Katie promised she would, and he got into his car and backed out of the driveway.

"Well, I'll see the two of you in before I head out," Buck said.

Katie walked up beside him and rested her hand in the crook of his arm as they made their way to the front door. "Thank you again for taking care of us, Buck. It's nice to have good friends." She smiled.

"I'll second that," Randy said. "Really nice."

They went upstairs to secure Katie's room, making sure the windows in her bedroom, bathroom, and closet were closed and locked, and the curtains were tightly drawn so no one could see in.

"I'm going to feel like a prisoner in here now," she said, growing frustrated. "I always have my windows open for fresh air and my curtains open for sunlight. I'll miss waking up to that in the mornings."

"I know, Peach, but it won't be forever." Randy put his arm around her. "Just until they catch this creep."

"I'll stay outside in my truck for a little while just to make sure no one comes around," Buck said.

"Thank you, Buck." Katie hugged them both. They headed downstairs and she closed her door to get ready for bed.

The next morning was overcast and dreary, matching Katie's mood. At the kitchen table, she slumped in her chair and rested her head in her hand. Even the smell of freshly brewed coffee couldn't entice her to move.

Randy walked in and sat down across from Katie. "What's wrong

50

with my girl?" he said. "You're still in your robe, you haven't fixed your coffee, and you're sitting there sulking. That's not at all like you, Peach."

Katie sighed. "Yeah, I know, Daddy." She slowly stood up and walked over to the counter to pour a cup of coffee. Then she turned around and frowned at her father. "I was lying in bed last night, and I couldn't help but think that this is how it's going to be from now on. Closed curtains, drawn blinds, not even able to sit on the porch at night in my favorite rocking chair, looking at the stars and hearing the crickets chirping and the animals out in the field."

Randy walked over to her and leaned against the counter. "Katie," he said, taking her hand, "your safety is what matters to me the most. It will be an inconvenience, I know, but we need to do what's best for you. And right now, this is what's best."

"I know, Dad." She grabbed her favorite mug from the cabinet and filled it with coffee. "Maybe I will still go to California with Matt tomorrow and stay for a little while."

"Well, if that's what you want to do, I'll miss you, but I will support it."

She smiled. "I'll miss you too, Daddy, but we can always text each other or call."

"You're right, Peach, and we can send those goofy pictures to each other, too. What do you call them again?"

"Are you talking about emojis?" She chuckled.

"Yeah, those. We can send each other emojis." He winked. "Well, Buck will be here soon. You go get ready. I'll start making breakfast for us."

When Katie came back downstairs, she walked into the living room and stood in front of the bay window to bask in the view for a few minutes. The sun was now peeking around the clouds, which made her feel a lot better. Buck's sweet-as-honey voice drifted down the hallway from the kitchen, and she couldn't help but smile.

She walked past the old bookcase in the hallway and leaned against the doorway to the kitchen, watching as her dad and Buck chatted and set the table for breakfast. Seeing them working as a team, so at ease with each other, filled her with a happiness she hadn't felt for a while now. Randy handed Buck three plates of food, and Buck brought them over to the table.

"Thanks, Buck. I'll give Katie a shout." Randy cupped his hands around his mouth and turned around. "Ka—"

He jumped when he saw Katie. "Oh! You scared me, Peach. I was just about to call for you. How long have you been standing there?"

51

She chuckled as she walked to the table. "Only long enough to see that my favorite breakfast food ever is sitting on the table." The steam rose from the biscuits and gravy in front of her as she sat down to take in the savory aroma.

"You seem to be in better spirits now," Randy said.

Buck looked at Katie with a raised brow. "Wanna talk about it?"

Katie took a sip of her orange juice and sighed. As they ate, she told Buck all about how she felt trapped, like she couldn't go outside or do anything she loved because she would feel watched and invaded.

Katie even went out on a limb and told him she was still considering going to California with Matt, but that because of the situation here, she might stay longer than just a few days. From the look on his face, she could tell Buck didn't like that idea at all.

She tried to reassure him. "It would only be until the police know a little more about what's going on here," she said. "I wouldn't stay there forever."

"Let's talk about this later," Randy said, clearing the table and bringing the dishes to the sink. "We need to meet Joe at the farmers' market soon."

He watched her open the car door, taking in every miniscule detail, like how her white jeans hugged her legs and how one of her light-brown sandals slid off her foot just a tad as she raised it gently to be as ladylike as possible climbing into the car. He imagined her auburn hair laid across her shoulders, smelling of honeysuckle on the vine. Her lips were like drops of sweet red wine on a hot summer's night. He longed to touch her soft skin, caress her face, look into her emerald eyes as these two other guys had done. Seething with the frustration he felt growing, he slipped away into the shadows, certain that this time, he'd left no trace of his presence.

The farmers' market was a delight for the senses. With Buck by her side, Katie walked around to every stand, sampling as many treats as she could: a hearty scoop of chocolate ice cream from a nearby creamery, raw honey drizzled on morsels of soft multigrain bread, flavorful slices of cheeses she'd never even heard of, juicy bites of bright-red watermelon.

After they made the rounds, a loud whistle came from off to the side of the market. Randy was waving them over. They walked over to Joe's truck, where he and Randy were standing.

"Joe's got a great idea, you guys," Randy said.

Joe smiled at them. "How's about we head over to the restaurant and have some fried chicken?"

"Sounds good to me, Joe," Buck said.

"As long as mashed potatoes and macaroni and cheese are involved, I'm in," Katie said.

"Tell you what," Joe said. "Help me load these boxes into my truck and I'll feed y'all." He motioned toward his purchases. "Just be careful with that top box. Those are eggs."

"What's in all these other boxes, Joe?" Randy asked, setting the box of eggs down softly in the bed of the truck.

"Mondays are when I stock up on bacon, fresh herbs, avocados, eggs, and a few other things," Joe said. "I like to use as many natural ingredients as possible when I cook. Now you know the secret to my delicious food!" He winked.

They met at Joe's Place and had a fantastic lunch together. "Thanks for coming today, guys," Joe said, dabbing the corner of his mouth with a napkin. "It sure was nice to have y'all here again."

Randy finished off his iced tea and sat the glass down on the table. "Honestly, it's where we should be every week, Joe. I can give you one excuse after another, but we should do this more often."

Buck nodded. "And with everything going on, this is one of the safest places to be."

Joe looked confused. "What do you mean, with everything going on?"

"If you gentlemen will excuse me, I must run to the little girls' room. Tell him the story, Daddy," Katie said as she stood up.

When Katie came back, Joe was shaking his head. "It's a shame you can't even go outside your own home without fear of something happening."

"True story, Joe," she said, "and I would agree. Shameful indeed."

53

The others stood up, and Randy thanked Joe for lunch.

"You're more than welcome," he said. "And if you guys need anything, don't hesitate to ask. I'll be glad to help."

CHAPTER NINE

Roses

As they walked up to the house after eating at Joe's, Katie saw a single white rose lying on the front steps. Katie looked at Randy, and Randy looked at Buck, who looked back at Katie.

"There's a note attached," Randy said, reaching down to pick it up.

You're as innocent as the white rose signifies.
A pure heart and a kind soul, that's why everyone loves you so much,
that's why I love you so much.

A tingle ran up Katie's spine and back down again. She shivered.

"You guys know what this means, right?" she asked. Randy and Buck stared at each other, each waiting for the other to answer.

"It was a rhetorical question, guys," Katie said. "It means I officially have a stalker. And it also means this fool is crazy enough to come right up to our porch. Who's to say he won't try to break in next time? It also means I won't be going to California. I am staying here to protect my family and defend our home!"

Buck reached out and touched Katie's arm. Before he could say anything, she cut him off. "This is our home, and I will not let it be invaded by some crazy person." She walked over to the front door. "I may look sweet, and like this note says, I might look innocent, but right now I am nothing but angry." She flung the door open, and it hit the inside wall with a loud crack.

Randy and Buck stood watching, eyes wide.

Randy broke the silence. "She's got the innocence of a child, but she's a spitfire when she's angry," he said. "Just like her momma." They walked inside.

Late that evening, after Buck had left and Randy had gone to bed, Katie slipped into her powder-blue, silk pajamas and walked downstairs to fix herself a mug of hot cocoa. Then she wrapped a blanket around herself and sat on the couch, gazing at the stars through the living room window. Below, the woods that surrounded the house glowed in the bluish light of the moon.

After finding that rose on the porch, Buck and her father made her promise not to go outside by herself. But she longed to be out there, sitting on the porch swing and enjoying the quietness of the evening with her hot cocoa. She knew she was safer inside, and she certainly didn't want her dad and Buck upset at her, but the thought of gently rocking on that swing in a warm summer night's breeze beckoned to her.

The temptation only grew stronger. *Well, maybe I'll just take a peek outside.* She tiptoed to the foot of the stairs and heard faint snores coming from her dad's room. A smile tickled the corner of her mouth. It reminded her of when she was a little girl, sneaking downstairs on Christmas to catch a glimpse of Santa Claus. She walked to the front door and placed her hand over the doorknob.

She hesitated. Her conscience was telling her—no, screaming at her—not to go outside. It would be the right thing to turn around and go back to the couch, or even better, upstairs to bed. But she didn't want to do that. Being in her room with all the curtains drawn and not being able to open the windows anymore felt suffocating. For several minutes she wrestled with her thoughts, looking back at the couch, then the front door, then back at the couch again.

No, she finally declared in her mind. *I'm tired of being a prisoner in my own home. I just need to prove that nothing will happen when I go outside. Then they'll see, and I can go out more often.*

Katie ever-so-quietly cracked the door open, but didn't close it all the way so the click wouldn't wake her dad. She crept over to the swing at the end of the porch and grimaced at the creaking noise the wood made and the squeak of the chains as she sat down. Finally, she was outside. She took a long breath of the evening air, then looked up at the beautiful, star-filled sky and did her best to capture the bright stars with her phone camera. Smiling and filled with such peace, she hummed a tune as she took shot after shot of the midnight sky.

From inside the thicket, he watched her sit down on the porch swing. Score. He had been hoping to catch half a glimpse of her slender silhouette as she

passed by her window, but here she was on the porch, in full view. Her gorgeous auburn locks spilled like a waterfall over the back of the swing, and her humming brought him a sense of calm. He couldn't wait to hold her, kiss her soft, warm lips, feel her arms around him as he embraced her petite body and held her close. Just the thought made his heart race and his hands quiver. He took a step closer to the edge of the brush.

∽

The loud crack of a branch jarred Katie out of her tranquil state. She jumped up and screamed. *That was way too loud to be just an animal. There's a person in those trees.* Her hands trembled. Frozen with fear, she couldn't even move her head to scan her surroundings, but even if she could, it was too dark to see anything.

Randy burst out the front door.

"Daddy—"

He ran over to Katie and took her in his arms. "It's all right, darlin'. What were you doing out here?" She broke down and sobbed as he held her.

"Aww, you're shaking, Peach. I'm here. You're safe. You're safe now. Let's get inside."

Randy locked and deadbolted the door, then ran into the living room and closed the curtains.

Katie plopped down on the couch while Randy went into the kitchen to phone the police. He dialed the emergency number. "Yes, this is Randy Calhoun. We have a situation at our house, and we need someone here immediately, please." Randy explained what had taken place.

After he hung up, he grabbed a blanket and wrapped it around Katie.

He sat down next to her and put his hand on her back. "What were you thinking going outside, honey?"

Katie took a deep breath, then exhaled. She was starting to calm down.

"I just don't want to be stuck in here like a prisoner, Daddy. I'm not the one in the wrong here, so why should I have to be locked away?" She snuggled closer to her father.

Randy wrapped his strong arms around her. "We'll get this figured out, Peach, and then you'll have your freedom back." He leaned his head on hers.

Several minutes later, bright headlights lit up the frosted glass of the front door. A loud knock followed, and Randy got up to answer the door.

"We've got an officer looking around outside the house right now," Sergeant Haskins said as he shook Randy's hand.

Randy invited him into the kitchen, and the two men took a seat at the table. Katie offered the sergeant a cup of coffee, which he politely declined.

He looked over at Katie and opened his notepad. "Now, tell me exactly what happened tonight, Katie."

Katie was nervous about telling him what she had done. Yesterday, it was he who had been the most adamant about her staying inside after dark, and here she was going against what amounted to direct orders from a police sergeant. It was almost like getting caught skipping school and having to go to the principal's office—or worse, breaking a window with a baseball and having to tell your parents what you had done. Her conscience was eating her up, and her lip quivered as she spoke.

"Well, I just wanted to go sit outside on the swing for a few minutes and take pictures of the sky," she said. "I had been looking out the window in the living room, but it just wasn't the same. When you're raised on a farm, you want to be outside practically all the time. As I was taking pictures of the sky, I heard the loud crack of a branch. And when I say loud, I mean it was loud."

Sergeant Haskins looked up from his notepad. "So, you don't think it could have been from an animal?"

"Not unless this animal was Bigfoot," she replied. "I was so startled at the sudden noise, I screamed and froze, and that's when Dad came running downstairs."

"Randy, did you happen to see anything?"

Randy stepped away from the counter and moved toward them. "No, I didn't see anything. We didn't stay outside long enough for me to see anything, honestly. I just took Katie straight inside."

An officer walked into the kitchen as Katie was finishing her statement. Sergeant Haskins's attention was diverted to something the officer was holding in his hand.

"This white petal was found next to some more black string, sir,"

58

the officer said.

Sergeant Haskins took the petal and the string and looked at Randy. "Do you guys have any white flowers around here?"

They both looked at each other, realizing they had both forgotten to mention the "gift" they had found.

"I'm so sorry, Sergeant Haskins," Randy said. "With everything that just happened, we completely forgot to tell you. A white rose was found lying on our front steps when we got back home from church this afternoon. There was a note attached to it as well."

Sergeant Haskins raised one eyebrow. "Really? Would you still happen to have the rose and the note?"

"They're in the dining room," Katie said, standing up from her chair. "I'll go get them."

"We may be able to get a print off the stem or even the paper that the note was written on," Sergeant Haskins said. "This could be our first good lead."

Randy sat down at the table. "I hope we didn't contaminate it or mess it up in any way by touching it."

Before the sergeant could answer, Katie walked in and handed him the rose and note. He looked them over and dropped them into a plastic bag.

"I'm sure it didn't mess anything up, but we'll take your prints just so we can tell whose are whose. Then we'll send this bag to the lab for analysis."

"When did you want to do the prints, sir?" Katie asked. "I will have to get Buck back over here if you need them tonight."

Sergeant Haskins looked at his watch. "Well, at this late hour, it won't really do any good to wake everyone up. The lab doesn't open until seven, so we can just have you guys come down to the station in the morning and have them done." He smiled. "I'll have a patrol car stay on the premises tonight to keep an eye out."

"Thank you so much," Katie said, shaking his hand. "That will make me feel a lot better."

The phone call Buck received that morning was not one he expected to get. Generally, whenever Katie was on the other end of the line, he was elated, but this time he was angry. He threw on his jeans and an old, gray tee shirt and drove over to their house.

On the way, he couldn't stop thinking about what could have happened had this nutjob of a man gotten his hands on her. He was angry at her for going out that late at night, especially after what they had found on the porch, but at the same time, he just wanted to hold her and feel her in his arms, knowing she was okay.

He pulled into the driveway and got out of his car. The chirp of his car alarm brought Katie and Randy out of the house. He ran up to Katie and held her in his arms.

"I'm so glad you're okay," Buck said. "What were you thinking? I'd be lost with you."

He loved how she felt in his arms. The warmth of her body against his and the feel of her heartbeat comforted him.

Then Katie stepped back. "Wait," she said, "did you just say you would be lost without me?" Her eyes searched his as she stood facing him.

"Look, I was angry when you told me what had happened. But I was also scared. The fact that you went out despite your best judgement made me angry, but the fact that that lunatic was so close to you and could have grabbed you and done God knows what with you scared the hell out of me."

Buck looked around, then took a deep breath. "I love you, Katie Marie Calhoun. I love you to the ends of the earth and back, okay? And my life wouldn't be the same without you in it. Please, please don't do that again."

∽

For a few seconds, neither Katie nor Randy spoke. Katie didn't know what to say, and she was guessing her father didn't either. All she knew was this whole thing with Buck and Matt was getting really complicated.

"Let's go inside," Randy finally said, laying his hand on Buck's shoulder. "Then, we'll fill you in on what the sergeant told us."

Katie fixed a pot of coffee, took a pitcher of lemonade out of the refrigerator, and sat them both on the table.

"So," Buck said, "this weirdo left a white rose petal and the same black string that was found the first time?"

"That's right," Randy said, pouring himself a lemonade.

"It makes me wonder if he even left yesterday or if he was just lying in wait," Buck said. "So what do we have to do?"

"Well," Katie said, taking a seat at the table, "the sergeant would like us to go to the station and have our prints taken, so when they examine the note and the stem of the rose, if any prints are found, they can compare them and rule ours out."

"That's a good idea," Buck said. He motioned toward the front door. "Shall we?"

That evening, Matt came over for dinner. They sat around the kitchen table, sipping peach iced tea and brainstorming the next steps for assuring Katie's safety. The more they talked, the more frustrated she became.

She couldn't take it anymore. "Why me?" she blurted out. "Why me? I mean, I know we live in a small town and all, but there *are* other women out there. Aaaargh. I don't mean I want any other woman to—"

"There may be other women out there, but none of them are as beautiful as you," Matt said, pushing the corn on his plate around with his fork.

Buck cleared his throat and got up from the table. "Little boys' room," he muttered, and disappeared down the hallway.

Matt looked over at Katie and took her hand. "Why don't you come back to California with me? That would more than ensure your safety because you wouldn't even be here."

Katie looked at her dad and then at Matt. She couldn't shake Buck's profession of love from earlier in the day. She knew, however, that she would need to make a decision soon because Matt was leaving in the morning.

"I'm so torn on what to do," Katie said. "What if the police need me for something and I'm not here? Or what if this crazy guy goes after Dad?"

Buck walked back in. "Oh, you don't have to worry about your dad, sweetheart. I'll be here to take care of him." He sat down at the table. "But first, fill me in. I missed it. Where are you going?"

Matt answered for her. "I think she should come to California with me for a while, Buck. At least until this whole mess blows over."

CHAPTER TEN

Beach Trip, Or...

Katie woke up the next morning to the sound of their rooster, Tom, crowing from a fencepost behind the house. He was extra loud today, or at least it seemed that way to her. She pulled the white down comforter back over her head and sighed deeply, hoping Tom would leave her in peace.

Cock-a-doodle-doooooooo! No such luck.

"Silly old bird," she muttered to herself, throwing the covers off. She needed to get up anyway. Her suitcase was packed for her trip to California, and Matt would be here in an hour or so to pick her up.

She pulled her hair back into a ponytail, and had just sat down on the edge of the bed to put her shoes on, when there was a knock on her bedroom door.

"Katie? It's me, Buck."

"Come in!"

Buck walked in with a thermos of coffee. She smiled when she noticed it was the thermos she'd purchased on her last trip to the beach. Swirls of blue and white covered the cup with "Relax" in big, bold letters on the front. He poured a cupful of steaming hot coffee for her.

"What's the occasion, Buck Brady? You trying to tell me something?" She laughed.

"Well, maybe." He returned her smile and gazed into her eyes. "Depends on if you feel like listening or not."

If he really was trying to tell her something, she didn't know what it was. She cocked her head sideways and looked at him. "Just what are you plotting, sir?"

He erupted in laughter and reached for her hand. "Follow me and you'll see."

Buck led her down the staircase, sliding her hand along the soft, brown wood of the railing as they descended. At the bottom of the stairs, he told her to close her eyes. She threw him a suspicious glance.

"Trust me," he said. "Would I ever let anything happen to you?"

She knew he wouldn't. In fact, she trusted him almost as much as

63

she trusted her own father. Buck guided her to the kitchen table and sat her down in one of the chairs.

"Keep your eyes closed," he said. "No peeking."

She was filled with the excitement of a child on Christmas. With her eyes closed, her other senses took in the scent of lilies, the sizzle of bacon, the clinking of silverware on the table.

"Okay, you can open your eyes now."

Katie opened her eyes and grinned. On the plate in front of her were all her favorites: scrambled eggs—still steaming—fresh strawberries and blueberries, toast with apple butter, and three strips of bacon. The plate was blue and white, with raised images of dolphins, starfish, and coral. Like the thermos, it was a souvenir from her trip to Virginia Beach.

"Aww, my favorite plate." She smiled.

Buck had even brought over fresh lilies, arranged them in a vase, and set them in the middle of the table.

She looked at all the yummy food and the beautiful flowers. His attention to detail was stupendous. She was so touched that he had done all this for her. He must have been here before the sun was up preparing it all. She bit into one of the bright-red strawberries.

"They were picked this morning," Buck said. "The eggs are fresh from the hens as well. And your bacon—well, we won't talk about that." He chuckled.

"I appreciate that," she said, chomping into a strip of bacon.

Breakfast was scrumptious. When she finished, she almost felt sad that there wasn't any more left. Buck told her not to get up, then cleared the table himself and set all the dishes in the sink.

As Buck cleaned up, Katie noticed the sun was casting a strange shadow on the kitchen floor. Wondering what could be causing it, she went out onto the back porch and saw her dad in the field, leaning on a fencepost. He waved and yelled good morning, then pointed behind her.

There it was, the reason for the shadow: a humongous flag, attached to the flagpole on the side of the house, whipping in the wind. On the flag was the image of a beach with two turquoise Adirondack chairs sitting in the sand, facing the ocean.

She thought of her upcoming trip to the west coast and smiled. But that thought quickly turned to guilt as she realized Buck probably wanted to take her to the beach today. She hadn't even told him she'd decided to go with Matt to California. He'd find out soon enough, though, when Matt showed up.

64

She leaned against the railing of the covered porch and gazed off into the distance, thinking about how to break the news to Buck. The warm wind caressed her face, blowing a few stray hairs into her eyes, which she brushed away.

The screen door opened, and Buck walked over to where Katie was standing. He leaned against the railing and the two stood in silence as they stared out at the vast fields of the farm.

They both spoke at the same time.

"Buck, I—"

"So, what do you say, Katie? Wanna take a ride to the beach with me?" He looked over at her. "It'll be a long drive, but it'll be fun. And a much-needed break. Plus, who doesn't want to put their feet in the water and reconnect?"

"I would love to, Buck, but I—"

"Before you say no, Katie, your dad and I already took care of all your chores this morning. I just wanted you to be able to spend the day with me."

She desperately wanted to go to the beach with Buck. But her suitcase was sitting in her room, packed and ready to go to California, and Matt was probably on his way over. Now, knowing Buck had finished all her chores for her this morning brought a fresh wave of guilt.

The door opened, and Randy came out onto the porch. He gave Buck a firm pat on the shoulder. "Thanks for helping me with those chores today, champ. It wasn't much to do, but I'll make sure you're taken care of."

Buck looked back at Randy and tipped his hat. "It was no problem at all, sir."

Katie loved how Buck made her father's life so much easier. For her, it was important to know her dad could relax as much as possible.

A loud knock came from the front door, and Randy stepped back inside to answer it. *That must be Matt*, she thought. Now was the time to tell Buck what was going on.

She took his hand. "Buck, can I talk to you?"

Randy had been sworn to secrecy about Katie's decision to go to California, because Katie wanted to be the one to tell Buck. He felt bad that Buck had even offered to help finish her chores, but stopping him would have meant spilling the beans.

He greeted Matt at the front door and led him out to the back porch where Katie was talking to Buck. He knew what their conversation was about and could see that Buck's demeanor had completely changed. He looked like someone had punched him in the gut. The usual sparkle was gone from his eyes.

Katie reached for Buck's hand, but he pulled it away and turned around. When he saw Matt, he glared at him as he rushed back into the house.

❧

"Buck, wait!" She turned and ran after him, but by the time she got to the front door, he was already hopping into his truck. His wheels spun as he tore out of the driveway, leaving a cloud of dust that settled mostly on Matt's car. She walked out onto the driveway.

As he sped onto the main road, she saw Buck slam the steering wheel with his hand. She knew how much he must be hurting. He had planned a road trip to the beach, arrived early, done her chores, and made her breakfast. She felt like she had let him down. *I should have told him sooner*, she thought. But it had been a last-minute decision, and what's more, Buck knew she was thinking about going to California. She just had no idea Buck would do all that for her, and today of all days.

"Buck didn't seem too happy. Did I walk in in the middle of something?"

She turned around. Matt was standing in the doorway, swinging his keys around his finger.

"I didn't have a chance to tell him I was going with you today, and he just found out," Katie said. "Well, we'd better go soon if we want to catch our flight. Matt, would you mind bringing my suitcase down from my room?"

Randy appeared in the doorway and walked over to Katie. He put his arm around her shoulder. "I know you're hurting, Peach, but I really think that you are doing the right thing for your safety."

66

"You're right, Daddy," she said. "I guess this is it. I'll be back soon. Please stay safe and don't go out after dark." She gave him a long hug.

Matt came back with Katie's suitcase and Randy shook his hand. "You take care of her, now," he said. "She is my everything."

"I will, sir. You have my word."

Randy opened the car door for her, and she climbed inside. "Call me when you get there, Peach. I love you."

She unrolled the window and waved as they drove away.

※

Randy waved until they were out of sight, then let out a ragged breath. The last few days had been exhausting, and he knew he wouldn't be able to rest until this situation was resolved.

He needed a few items from Merriman's, so he jumped into his truck and headed to town.

Frank Merriman was wiping down the counter when Randy walked in. Hearing the bell jingle, Frank looked up and beamed.

"Hey there, Randy," he said, reaching across the counter to shake Randy's hand. "Long time no see! What brings you in here today and not Miss Katie?"

"It's kind of a long story, Frank." He quickly explained what had been going on over the past few days.

"Whew, that's scary. It sounds like you and Katie are doing what's best for her safety, though. And you've got the top guy on the case. Sergeant Haskins knows what he's doing, so I'm sure everything will be just fine." He smiled. "Hey, off topic, but I hired a new guy a few weeks ago. Would you like to meet him? He's a really good worker, and I thought if you ever needed a helping hand with any projects on the farm, he'd be great."

Randy walked alongside him to the back of the store. "You haven't hired anyone new for a long time, Frank!"

"Yeah, I know," Frank said as he pushed open the double doors of the back room. "I really should've hired someone sooner, but he's been a great help to me." He chuckled and looked around the room for his new hire. "His name is Tate Stevens."

❧

From behind the shelves, he watched them talking and carrying on. Why had he come in and not her? She hadn't come here in a while. He wanted to see her face, hear her laugh, and smell her sweet scent as she passed by.

❧

Frank called for him over the loudspeaker. After a minute, the double doors swung open, and in walked Tate. He shuffled over to where Frank and Randy were standing and gave them a quick nod. His black, button-up shirt was coming untucked from his tan work pants. He looked tired.

"Tate, this is Randy Calhoun. He's a real good friend of mine. I think you might have met his daughter, Katie."

Randy extended his hand and Tate shook it. "Nice to meet you," Tate said, not making eye contact. "Your daughter is very pretty."

"Thank you."

"Well, if you'll excuse me," Tate said, "I gotta get back to work." He walked off.

When Tate was gone, Frank shrugged and lowered his voice. "As you can see, he has his quirks, but he does a good job. I can't complain."

They chatted a little more on their way back to the front. Randy checked out, said goodbye to Frank, and left.

CHAPTER ELEVEN

Airports and Hot Wings

Matt and Katie got to the airport without much time to spare before boarding. Matt could tell Katie was excited—almost as excited as the day in high school when they snuck away to the fair. He'd met her at the back fence, and they sped off on his motorcycle as fast as its wheels could take them. She laughed at the powdered sugar he had on his nose from the funnel cake, and he laughed at the way she begged him to take her on the Ferris wheel again before they had to go.

"Sir?" The security agent's voice snapped him out of his trance. "May I see your boarding pass?"

"Uh, yeah. Sorry." Embarrassed, he pulled up his boarding pass, fumbled for his ID, then moved ahead in line to go through the security screening.

After they had boarded the plane and were settled in their seats, Katie looked over at Matt. "You were pretty dazed back there at security," she said. "What were you so deep in thought about?"

"Oh, it was just ... do you remember the time we snuck away to the fair?" he asked, taking her hand.

"Of course," she said. "That was so much fun. I jumped on the back of your bike and we were gone like the wind!" She giggled. "I never thought we'd get there and back without getting caught."

෨

Katie looked down at her hand in his. His hands were soft, much different than Buck's. Buck's hands were tan, his palms calloused from working on the farm, while Matt's were properly manicured with no signs that he worked outside. The hand sanitizer he had put on before boarding gave off a light scent of lavender.

A flight attendant walked by to make sure their seat belts were fastened before takeoff, then made her way up front to present the

69

safety instructions.

Katie squealed as the plane took off and the first burst of gravity pinned her to the seat. Once they reached altitude, she leaned back a little in her seat and stared out the window. She wondered if this was the view her mom had from Heaven, and if she spent her days looking down on them. Feeling sleepy, she leaned her head against Matt's shoulder and closed her eyes.

☙

"Hey, Buck, how are you?" Randy said into the phone as he pulled a beer out of the fridge. "I was wondering if you'd like to come have dinner tonight and watch the game. It's all-you-can-eat wing night at Joe's Place, so I went and picked some up." He walked into the living room and set the chicken wings and all the fixings on the coffee table in front of the TV.

"Sounds like a grand idea to me," Buck said. "Sure beats sitting home alone."

Randy sighed as he looked around at his empty home. "I feel the same way, bud. See you soon."

☙

Buck slipped his shoes on and walked past the kitchen counter, where Katie had stood just the other day. He caught a whiff of honeysuckle and lilacs and whirled around thinking Katie would be there, only to see emptiness instead.

"Wow. Get a grip, Buck," he said to himself. He grabbed his keys, turned off the lights, and walked out the door.

When he arrived at the farm, his headlights swept over a shiny object lying on the ground near the porch. He parked and walked over to take a closer look at it. In the glare of his phone's flashlight, he saw it was a thin piece of metal.

And it was covered in blood.

He gasped and ran to the front door. It was locked. "Damn it!"

Buck said under his breath. He rang the doorbell and banged on the door as hard as he could. "Randy!" he yelled. "Are you in there? Open the door!" With each passing second, Buck thought the worst. He envisioned himself breaking down the door and finding Randy lying inside, bleeding and barely alive. He yelled again for Randy, ringing the doorbell again and again.

The door flew open, and there stood Randy. "What in tarnation are you doing, boy?" He looked annoyed. "Are you okay? Is somebody after you?"

Buck stepped back in shock. "Randy! You're ... not dead."

"Well, of course not. Am I supposed to be?" He chuckled, still looking puzzled.

"No, I just ..." Buck leaned forward and placed his hands on his knees, trying to catch his breath. "Come take a look at what I found over here." He showed Randy the broken piece of metal. "It looks like the blade of a knife with blood all over it, don't you think?" He looked at Randy.

"You're right. It looks like the broken end of a small pocketknife. Really strange. Let me run inside and get something to put it in." He came back and used a paper towel to drop the blade into a plastic sandwich bag.

The two headed inside, and Buck plopped down on the sofa. "Quite the spread you have here, Randy," he said, looking at all the food he had set out.

Randy handed him a beer and patted his shoulder. "I figure you can't go wrong when you have good wings, a good game on, and a good friend to share it with."

That made Buck smile. He thought a lot of Randy and was glad he felt the same about him. He took a sip of his beer and set it down on the coffee table.

"Who's winning?" Buck asked, picking up a paper plate and filling it with wings.

"All tied up in the bottom of the third inning." Randy grabbed the remote and turned up the volume. "Braves just scored a homer against the Orioles."

"Braves shmaves," Buck said. He knew that slam would get Randy all worked up. Out of the corner of his eye he could see Randy staring over at him, and he hid a smile as he took another swig.

"You know the front door works both ways and I can let you right back out, don't ya?" Randy said. "Your birds ain't no better, son."

"Them's fightin' words right there, Randy."

They both burst out laughing.

A jolt of turbulence startled Katie out of her peaceful sleep. Matt wrapped his arm around her.

"It's okay, Kat. Just a bit of shaking," he said. "Nothing to worry about."

She yawned and stretched and tried to wake up. She cleared the hair out of her face and rubbed the sleep from her eyes.

"Boy, I really conked out," she said, looking around. "Are we almost there?"

Matt moved his arm out from around her and opened the window shade so she could see out.

"Yep. Just about to be home sweet home." He smiled.

The city was beautiful at dusk. Gazing out at all the lights made Katie imagine she was looking down on the stars.

Maybe this won't be too bad after all, she thought. In fact, she was getting excited about being in a new place. New sights, new smells, new faces, and new experiences awaited her.

The plane touched down and taxied to the airport terminal. She and Matt grabbed their belongings, said goodbye to the flight attendant at the door, and stepped off the plane. Arm in arm, they walked down the hall to baggage claim, where a familiar face was there to greet them.

Katie ran over to Matt's mom and hugged her. "I feel like it's been forever since I saw you last!" Katie said as she stepped back from her. She hadn't changed at all or even aged one bit. Tall and slender with strawberry blonde hair and blue eyes, she still smelled of the same sweet perfume.

"Maggie Fuller, a sight to behold," Matt said as he gave his mom a hug.

"It's good to see you too, son," she said, tousling his hair.

Maggie turned to face Katie. "Tell me, how is your dad?"

"He's doing pretty well. But there's a lot going on at home right now, which makes it kind of stressful." Katie reached into her purse. "That reminds me, I need to text him and let him know I got here safely."

"Go right ahead, dear. Matt told me some of the story when he called to let me know you'd be joining him." Maggie smiled. Her smile always put Katie at ease. "Let's get you some food and off your feet and we can talk more about it if you want."

Katie really didn't want to talk about it, but she knew Maggie would make her feel better about the situation. "I'd like that," she said.

∽

Randy and Buck finished their third beer and stepped outside to sit on the porch swing. With a warm breeze, they sat and looked at the stars. Buck took a deep breath. It sure was weird without Katie around. Her presence, her laugh, her energy. He missed her.

"You know, I love your daughter, sir," Buck said, glancing over at Randy.

Randy leaned forward and patted Buck's knee. "That's been pretty obvious to me," he said. "I know I haven't always been a proponent of your dating my daughter seeing as how you work for me, but I see how strong your love is for her. You look at her like ... uh ..." Randy's voice trailed off.

Buck looked over at Randy, wondering why he had suddenly fallen silent. Randy held his finger up to his lips and tilted his head to listen. A light rustle in the brush came from the side of the house. They looked at each other, then hurried inside and locked the door.

∽

That was a close call. Don't get caught, you idiot. Where is she, anyway? When is she coming back? Is she coming back at all?

CHAPTER TWELVE

Close Call

"Wow, what an amazing meal," Katie said as she took the last bite of her dessert. She sat back in her chair and let out a sigh, blowing a stray lock of auburn hair out of her face.

"How do you think I got my handsome figure?" a booming voice said from behind her. Russell Fuller, Matt's dad, walked into the dining room and gave Maggie's shoulder a light squeeze. "It wasn't from a lack of amazing meals, that's for sure."

"Oh, stop," she said, laughing. "How was work today, honey?"

"Just fine," he said, taking a seat in the empty chair beside Katie. "You look as lovely as ever, Katie. I heard you were coming to stay with us for a bit."

"Thank you, and yes," Katie said, looking over at Matt. "I was only going to be staying for a few days at first. But I talked it over with my dad, and with everything up in the air at home, we decided probably a couple of weeks would be best."

Russell reached over and patted her hand, which was resting on the table. "Please, stay as long as you need to. You know you're always welcome here."

Russell was a little heavier now, with a few gray strands peppering his light golden-brown hair. Laugh lines around his mouth and crow's feet at his eyes gave him a distinguished look that put Katie at ease and made her feel secure in his presence. He smelled of pine needles, almost like a freshly cut Christmas tree, which brought back a flood of memories. She'd never met anyone else with a scent like that.

He stood up and smiled. "Would anyone like some coffee or hot cocoa? I'd love a cup myself."

"No, sir," Katie said. "If it's okay with you, I really think I would like to go take a shower and hit the hay. It's been a long day, and I need to call my dad and let him know I'm all settled in."

Maggie walked over and hugged Katie. "You go right ahead and make yourself at home. See you in the morning."

As Katie walked up the stairs, she looked at all the pictures on the

75

wall. There was one of Matt when he was on the football team in middle school, one of the whole family at Christmas time, and one of the family enjoying a Thanksgiving meal. But the last one stopped her in her tracks. There in a rustic wooden frame was the last picture that she and Matt had taken together before they moved away. She had the same photo in a small frame on her dresser back home. They were leaning up against an old oak tree outside their house in Georgia. She remembered that day vividly, as if it had happened just yesterday. Her smile was peaceful, the love in her heart as real as rain, their relationship as strong as the tree they were leaning against. A lump welled up in her throat.

She walked down the hallway to the guest room that would be hers for the next couple of weeks. The bed looked as soft as a cloud, and she couldn't wait to slip into those cool sheets after a steaming hot shower. She opened her suitcase and took out some clean undergarments and her blue silk pajamas, then headed for the shower. As soon as the hot water hit her face, Katie finally relaxed.

∽

"I love her just as much as I always did," Matt was saying to his parents downstairs. "Being around her these past few weeks has made me realize that we still have 'it' inside of us."

"I sense a 'but' coming on," Russell said, taking a sip of his coffee.

Matt chuckled. "Yes. But ... there's another guy in the picture. They aren't dating or anything, but he's in love with her. I know he is. He looks at her the way I do."

"If I'm not mistaken," Maggie said, "there's a third guy in love with her, too. What about this man who's been making his presence known there?"

"They're investigating, but so far, nothing," Matt said. "And they might not find anything until something else happens."

"The biggest concern right now is her safety," Russell said.

"Exactly," Matt said. "That's why she's here. I want to make sure she's taken care of."

❧

Katie couldn't wait to get into bed. She dried off, got dressed, and walked back down the hall. In the bedroom, she peeled back the blankets, exposing the white cotton sheets. Her whole body relaxed as she slid her feet all the way down to the foot of the bed, the softness of the sheets and the fluffiness of the pillow inviting her to let all of her stress and anxiety go.

She took a deep breath, sent her dad a goodnight text, and drifted off to sleep.

❧

Randy bolted into the living room and closed all the curtains, while Buck took a seat on the sofa.

"What exactly did you hear, Randy?"

"I heard a rustling in the bushes on the side of the house. I mean, it could have been a raccoon or something, but I don't want to take any chances." Randy sat down in the armchair.

"This is just dumb now, Boss," Buck said, growing frustrated. "We can't go running inside over every little rustle and close ourselves in like prisoners because of this guy."

He ran over to the door, unbolted it, and stepped outside. Standing on the edge of the porch, he screamed into the blackness.

"I'm not afraid of you, you little punk! You hear me? You want to harass someone? Harass me! You want to mess with someone? Mess with me! Come out and show yourself, you little yellow-bellied coward!" He shook his fist.

It felt so good to let his frustration out. The animals all answered him in unison, so at least he knew someone had heard him.

"Are you out of your mind, Buck?" Randy yelled from the front door. "Get back in here!" Buck turned and headed back in, his face still red. Randy slammed the door behind him.

❧

He stepped out of the shadows. He had heard him loud and clear. Yellow-bellied coward? Punk? Oh, I'll harass you, all right.

He walked over to Buck's truck and took his knife out of his pocket. He flipped it open, but no blade appeared.

"Damn," he muttered under his breath. He had forgotten.

Earlier, he'd been just about to cut a stray thread from his shirt when a sudden noise startled him, and he sliced his hand. He dropped the knife, and when it hit the ground, the blade broke off and he couldn't find it.

"You're safe tonight, old girl," he said to the truck as he rubbed his hand across the hood. But he was surely going to see to it that each tire had a good-sized hole in it.

I'll show you who the yellow-bellied coward is. I'll show you who the punk is. He was so angry his whole body was shaking. He slipped back into the shadows.

❧

The next morning Buck rose early and fixed a pot of coffee. He had been so tired and angry last night that Randy suggested he stay over instead of trying to drive home in that state. Buck didn't mind. He would have gone home to an empty house anyway. Randy came out and joined him on the back porch, taking the seat next to him.

"We sure do have a lot to do today, huh, Buck?" Randy said.

"Yeah." Buck shifted in his chair, took a sip of coffee, and lowered his sunglasses a little. "I reckon we do."

Buck glanced over at Randy, then did a double take when he saw an ever-widening smile creeping across Randy's face.

"Let's not do any of it," Randy said. "Let's just feed these guys and not do anything else."

Buck didn't know what to make of what he had just heard. Up and taking a day off when there was work to be done wasn't something he expected to hear from Randy.

"Boss?"

"Look, we work hard all the time, right? Don't we deserve a cheat day, so to speak? This stuff will be here tomorrow, and the day after that, and the day after that. Let's find something else to do."

"I'm game." Buck took another sip of his coffee, certain Randy had lost his mind but excited about the prospect of hanging out with him away from the farm. "What did you have in mind, Boss?"

"Let's go down to the winery. It's been a long time since I've been there. It's only about ten miles down the road."

"The winery, Randy?"

Randy stared at him. "Don't act all funny, boy," Randy said, gazing out at the far reaches of his farmland. "I have a vision for this place, and I need to get some ideas. I have a whole lot of land here, as you know, and it's senseless to let it go to waste. Katie will need more than just some cows when I'm gone, which is why I want to build a vineyard on the farm."

Randy looked down and took a deep breath. "You know, Katie has always had a love for peaches, and her momma used to love a good glass of wine. Her mom and I spent many a night out on the front porch, and she would often look at me, smile, and hold up her wine glass. Almost like she was toasting to the life we'd built together. So I got to thinking, why not toast to that life by building a whole winery? We can produce several flavors of wine, and even make wine from peaches. I think that would be a great way to honor them both."

Buck nodded. "That's amazing, Randy. I think we need to put this plan into motion. Shall we? The sooner we feed these guys, the sooner we can head out." He stood up.

"Attaboy," Randy said, standing and patting Buck on the shoulder. They set out for the barn.

⤫

The sun was warm on Katie's face when she woke. She sprung from the bed and quickly made it up, then headed downstairs for breakfast, excited to start the day in this new place.

Katie had always loved the homey feel of their huge eat-in kitchen. This morning, the marble island was piled high with delicious-looking breakfast foods: eggs, bacon, sausage, French toast, pastries, and jam. And

79

Maggie was just setting a pot of hot coffee next to two carafes full of orange juice and apple juice.

"Wow," Katie said when she saw the spread. "I didn't know we were feeding royalty this morning." She giggled.

Matt walked in and kissed her cheek. "Well, we do have a princess in our midst."

"I hope you're hungry," Maggie said. "I guess I did get a little carried away. It's just that it isn't often we have company, and I remember how much you like breakfast. By the way, Katie, I love your outfit," she said, pointing to her teal tunic and white jeans.

"Thank you." She'd been sure to pack her cutest clothes.

Russell walked in. "Wow, honey," he said, winking at Maggie, "all you ever fix me is oatmeal." That made Katie laugh out loud.

"Then I guess you'd better eat up, Russell, and not get used to it." Maggie laughed.

"If anyone's free today, I would love to go out and see all the little stores in town," Katie said. She took a sip of her orange juice and started in on her bacon and eggs.

"There's a great little strip of stores we can go to," Maggie said, "just on the edge of town."

"Why don't you girls do that, and Matt and I can go out and do guy stuff?" Russell winked at Matt.

"Sounds great!" Katie said.

They cleared the dishes and Katie helped Maggie clean up before they headed out.

"There's also a nice little dress shop we can go to first if you want to," Maggie said, handing Katie a glass to dry and put away.

"I love summer dresses," Katie said. "They're not the best thing to wear working on a farm, mind you, but they are great to have for free days."

Maggie dried her hands and draped the blue, checkered dish towel over the oven handle. "Then that's where we'll go today. It's the first of many free days for you."

Matt sighed as his father drove them down the boulevard. "I want to do right by her, Dad."

Russell looked over at Matt and smiled. "I know you do, son. I know you do. You've been in love with her ever since we were living just down the street from her, and you held on even after we moved away."

While they were out together that day, Matt spent plenty of time lost in thought. Then, on the car ride home that evening, Matt looked over at Russell. "I finally figured it out, Dad. I know what I need to do."

CHAPTER THIRTEEN

Slow Tides and Slower Kisses

Katie and Matt sat on his back deck watching the sunset. Pinks and purples twirled around hues of light blue as if they were caught up in a passionate lover's dance. Matt picked up his glass of red wine and swirled it around.

"I have a great idea, Kat." Matt set his glass down and took her hand in his.

She looked at him, afraid his idea was going to be walking around town again. By now, she'd seen everything there, and her feet were sore from the concrete. She longed for the dirt and grass of the farm.

"What would that be, Matt?"

"Let's go to the beach and finish watching the sunset there." His eyes sparkled.

"Yes, I would love that!"

They had spent a couple of hours at the beach one day last week, and had vowed to return, but hadn't made it back yet. Katie got ready as quickly as she could, then practically ran out the door to hop in the car. She felt like a giddy child, but she couldn't help getting excited about simple things like going to the beach. As Katie had told Matt many times, she valued simplicity far more than extravagance.

Matt pulled into a parking lot near the beach. As soon as the car stopped, Katie flung the door open and got about halfway out before the seat belt, which she had forgotten to unhook, pulled her back in.

Matt roared with laughter. "That's one for the memory books, Kat, without a doubt!"

"I'm fine," she said, glaring at him. "Thanks for asking."

"Oh, come on. If that were me, would you have asked first and then laughed, or the other way around?" He got out and walked around to help her out of the car.

Once she was on her feet, she gave Matt a quick jab in the ribs and took off running.

"Last one there is a sandy crab!" she yelled.

The sand between her toes felt divine. The salty air kissed her cheeks and blew through her hair. Seagulls called to her from overhead. The echo of the waves crashing against the shoreline calmed her.

She stared out at the water, trying to picture all the life that lurked beneath. Sharks, whales, sea turtles, sea horses, and every fish imaginable, living down there together, just like humans lived up here. She found it fascinating how the surface of the water could look so tranquil yet bustle with life underneath.

Matt walked up behind her and wrapped his arms around her waist. She turned to face him with a twinkle in her eye.

"You, my dear sir, are the sandy crab!"

Still panting from running all the way down to the water, he took her hand and they walked along the beach. With each wave, sea foam gathered around their ankles, and as the water retreated, she almost felt as if she were going to fall. Watching each wave lap over the last mesmerized her, made her feel at ease. Made her feel ... at home.

"You know, Kat," Matt said, "if you moved here, you would have this all the time."

Katie turned to face him, then glanced back at the water. "As much as I love this place and the beauty it holds," she said, "too much of a good thing can eventually turn into a bad thing. I might grow tired of it and not appreciate it as much as I do now."

She looked down at the sand. During her time in California, she'd been asking herself what she should do, pick up where she left off with Matt or travel the new path to an unknown destination?

She'd been so confused, but now, it was becoming clear. For the first time since Matt had reappeared in her life, she was finally at peace about what she needed to do.

∾

Buck's neck seared under the late-morning sun, even with his Stetson on, as he and Randy walked from the pickup truck to the stately entrance of the vineyard. The grass out front was neatly cut, the landscaping impressive. A large, wooden sign greeted them at the entrance:

WHITE'S WINERY

What Buck saw when they walked inside overwhelmed him. Fields of grapes seemed to stretch for miles. Dozens of workers on ladders filled containers with the grapes they were picking.

"This looks like a lot of work, Randy," Buck said. "Are you sure we can do something like this at your place?"

"Well, sure," Randy said. "It is going to be a lot of work, but anything worth anything always is. I have plenty of land for something like this. Maybe not on the scale of this one, but at least half of it." Randy grabbed a handkerchief out of his pocket and dabbed his face with it. "Let's see if we can talk to the manager about what running a vineyard entails."

Randy pushed open a large, white door that led to a gift shop with a reception area. The scent of a grape candle greeted them as they walked up to the front counter. Buck dinged the bell near the register and a young woman, probably no older than Katie, walked out to greet them. She had a burgundy apron wrapped around her waist and a smile as pretty as a sunset.

"Can I help you gentlemen?"

"Yes," Randy said, "I own a farm a ways up the road, and I was hoping to speak with someone about what it takes to run a place like this." He set his hand on the counter and looked around.

"Of course," she said. "I'll get our manager for you." She turned and walked past a wooden display rack full of wines to a man with gray hair dressed in khakis and a blue, button-up shirt. She said something to him and motioned toward Randy and Buck. He came over.

"Greetings, gentlemen. My name is Mike Taylor," he said as he shook their hands. "I understand you're interested in starting your own winery?"

"Yes, sir," Randy said, explaining what he wanted to do.

Mike raised his eyebrows. "That sounds like a great project. And you already own a farm, so at least you know what hard work truly means." He chuckled.

"Absolutely," Buck chimed in. "Hard work is about all we do all day."

"Tell you what," Mike said. "We offer paid tours, but I've got a little free time right now. Why don't I bring you around the winery myself and show you a little bit more of how we operate behind the scenes?"

Mike took them on a grand tour of the winery. He first showed them around the gift shop, where all their wines, wine glasses, and wine bags were on display along with other merchandise such as cheeses and branded clothing. Mike talked about how the winery was founded, described the daily tasks involved in running the operation, and showed them the area where the grapes were processed, explaining in detail the steps to making the perfect bottle of wine.

Several times during the tour, Buck looked at Randy as though he'd gone plum mad. *How would we ever be able to do this?* he kept thinking.

But Randy remained resolute, even after learning more about what was involved. After the tour, they walked into the wine sampling room, where two glasses of red Moscato waited for them. Holding up his glass, Buck toasted Randy.

"To the only man I know who wants to start a whole new operation along with his other one, and have me be the only one working for him." Buck laughed and took a sip of wine.

Randy patted Buck on the shoulder. "This will be a lot of work, I know, but you won't be the only one working for me, bud. I wouldn't do that to you. You will, however, be second in command to me."

After finishing their wine, they thanked Mike for his time and walked out to the truck.

"Let's make a pit stop at Merriman's so I can grab something for dinner," Randy said as they pulled out of the winery parking lot.

Buck rubbed his stomach. "I'm all for that. Walking around a winery sure does make you hungry, and I couldn't eat many of those cheese samples. They almost reminded me of what my feet smell like after a day at your farm." He nudged Randy's shoulder and laughed.

Walking into the grocery store, Randy grabbed a cart and set about shopping for dinner.

He watched them walk in just as he had every so often these past few days. But where was she? Had she not returned? Night after night, he sat just out of sight at her bedroom window. Just watching, waiting, to see a light come on in her bedroom window, or some sign she was there. But nothing. He was growing restless. He wanted to see her face, hear her laugh, smell her sweet perfume. He wanted to touch her and feel her ivory skin against his. Feel her breath on his face as he pressed her body against his. But this was only a fan-

tasy. He knew it wouldn't come to pass. Why would she, a beautiful, angelic creature, want anything to do with him, a lowly grocery boy. He had plans, though. Plans to ensure his needs would be fulfilled.

⤸

"Hello, guys!" Frank said, spotting them admiring the fruit stand that was piled high with apples, oranges, and bananas.

"Hey, Frank," Buck said as he picked up several ruby-red apples and placed them in a bag. "These are beautiful fruits."

"Fresh stock this evening, Buck. My boy Tate just loaded the tables full."

"I see that," Randy said, then chuckled. "Looks like he was making sure he wouldn't have to come back to this table for a while."

"Yeah, he does pretty good." Frank leaned toward Randy and lowered his voice. "He's been a little on edge recently, though, and I just can't put my finger on why."

"How do you mean?" Randy asked.

"He's been real fidgety." Frank picked up an apple and rolled it around in the palm of his hand. "Or maybe distracted is a better word. Tate's a great worker. I just worry about him is all. We're like family here, so if something is going on with one of my employees, I like to help if I can." He set the apple back down.

"Well, you know how it was to be a young'un," Randy said. "Life isn't the easiest for them these days. I'm sure it's nothing to be concerned about."

"Yeah, I hope so. Well, Randy, let me know if you need anything." He shook Randy's hand and walked away toward the back of the store.

Randy looked around for Buck. "Now where did he—"

"Hey, Randy."

"Oh, there you are, Buck. I was just wondering where you'd gotten off to. Ready to go?"

⤸

87

Tate saw them coming and slunk back into the corner where he was stocking the pasta. He kept an eye on them as they made their way to the self-checkout, then followed them outside, gathering carts in the parking lot so they wouldn't suspect anything. That wasn't part of his job, but they wouldn't know that. All the while, he watched Buck out of the corner of his eye, longing to be in his shoes. His day would come. She would be his. Tate gave the truck a dirty look as it pulled away, then went back inside, leaving the carts behind, unaware that Buck had been watching his every move.

CHAPTER FOURTEEN

Desire

Buck poured the last glass of peach iced tea from the pitcher Katie had made before she left. It was only half a glass, but he wouldn't even try to make more. He only liked it the way she made it.

"We just scored a home run!" Randy shouted from the living room. Buck walked back in and sat down on the sofa.

"I really miss Katie," Buck said. "It feels like it's been so long since she left."

Katie had been calling regularly to let them know how she was doing, and Buck loved hearing the glee in her voice as she went on about the beach, the small, out-of-the-way shops, and the beautiful scenery out in California. She'd ask how things were going on the farm, how her favorite calf was doing, and what her father was eating while she was away.

"How is the whole stalker situation?" Katie had asked the day before. Randy put her on speakerphone so Buck could talk to her, too. "You know I love it here, but I miss my home, and I miss you guys." Her voice cracked. To Buck, it was clear she was homesick and ready to come home.

"Well, Peach, there really hasn't been any activity here since you left. It's been pretty quiet."

"I love you, Daddy," she said in a weak voice at the end of their conversation.

After the game, Randy and Buck carried their dishes into the kitchen and set them in the sink.

Randy looked at Buck. "Son, I know how you feel. I miss her, too. Right now more than ever."

"I love her, Randy, and it's killing me that she's so far away." Buck turned around and walked toward the front door.

Randy followed Buck onto the porch. The night was silent save for the faint sound of chirping crickets, the sky pitch black save for the stars.

"She'll be back before you know it, Buck. We just have to make sure everything is safe for her return." Randy tilted his head back to look up at the stars.

Just then, a pair of headlights turned into the driveway. The pop

89

of the gravel under the tires got louder as the vehicle approached the front of the house. Buck looked over at Randy, hoping he'd know who it was, but Randy just shrugged.

The engine of the black SUV shut off and the door opened. Sergeant Haskins, dressed in his uniform, stepped out and walked up to them.

"Good evening, gentlemen," he said, extending his hand. "I was hoping I would find you still up."

Buck gave the sergeant a mushy handshake that was about as weak as his knees. "Has something happened, Sergeant?" he asked. He was terrified to hear the answer, fearing Katie would have to stay away even longer.

"I didn't mean to alarm you by showing up like this. I should have called first, but I happened to be driving by on my way home. I just wanted to see how you were doing and ask you how Katie was holding up."

Buck breathed a long sigh of relief, and he could see Randy relaxing, too.

"I talked to her the other day," Randy said, "and aside from being really homesick, she's doing all right."

"I know you guys will be glad to have her come back soon."

"You got that right, Sarge," Buck said. "Randy's cooking is nothing like hers." He patted his belly and they all chuckled.

"There's no doubt about that," Randy said, taking a seat in one of the rocking chairs. "How are things in the investigation?"

"So far, it's been quiet," the sergeant said. "No other activity has been reported. It's possible that whoever this is knows she's not here and has given up."

Buck lit up. "Does that mean she can come back then?"

He could see it in his mind: a huge welcome-home party with balloons, cake, a good old-fashioned barbecue, and everyone Katie knew in attendance. He'd finally get to hold her in his arms, feel her breath on his face, and kiss her soft lips, knowing she was home to stay.

"I would say wait a little longer just to be on the safe side," Sergeant Haskins said. "We can't be too hasty and jeopardize her safety. I know you guys want her home, but we have to do what's best for her right now. If this person has been watching her and knows that she left, he may be keeping tabs on her, waiting patiently for her to come back."

Buck sighed. He hadn't thought of that. *What if this person knows she left?* he asked himself. *What if, when she comes back, it all starts again?*

"Well, I can't say I'm exactly thrilled to hear that," Randy said. "But I know you're right. We must keep her safety in mind and do what is best for her."

Buck had a dull ache in his chest. He longed to see her face, touch her soft, ivory skin.

"How much longer would you suggest?" Buck asked.

"Maybe another few weeks just to be safe." Sergeant Haskins turned and walked toward his vehicle. "I will keep you guys up to date on what's going on. Until then, stay strong and remember that what you're doing is the right thing."

❧

As the sergeant drove off, Randy glanced over at Buck and saw the faraway look in his eyes. He wondered what he was thinking about at that moment. But Randy didn't have to think too hard. He had the same look in his own eyes whenever he thought of his wife.

❧

Tate lurked just out of sight and watched the SUV pull out of the driveway. Patience is key, he told himself. Her bedroom window has been dark for too long, but soon my time with her will come. I just have to stay calm and keep it together. Not like poor little Buck, who's starting to lose his grip without her here. Now he knows how I feel. He reached into his pocket and unfolded a picture of Katie that he'd taken from Frank Merriman's office. He stared at her beautiful face. I've longed for you for an eternity, my dear, and soon, you will be in my grasp. He stifled a laugh.

CHAPTER FIFTEEN

California Dreamin' or Farm Livin'?

Katie lay awake in bed, staring at the faint glow of the moon on the ceiling. Even though she was exhausted from spending a day at the beach, walking around town, and eating delicious food, she couldn't sleep. She missed home. She missed the musky smell of the barn, the hay, and the animals. She missed the sweetness of her daddy's cologne. She missed the radiant smile that awaited her every morning as she opened the door to greet Buck.

Frustrated, Katie threw the covers off and walked over to the window. The street below and all the houses in this posh neighborhood sat in darkness. Back home, her own bedroom window gave her a sweeping view of majestic mountains and the lush, green fields of their farm.

"I am not a city girl, that's for sure," Katie whispered, wrapping her arms around her shoulders.

She sighed and walked back to bed. Tears came as she flipped through pictures of her dad and Buck and the farm. Crying into her pillow, she imagined herself on the farm, sitting on the porch with her daddy, drinking iced tea while he sipped a cup of coffee.

Out of nowhere, Buck appeared in front of her with that wide, irresistible grin. She had missed him so much it hurt. His biceps bulged out of his white tee shirt, and his Wrangler jeans, tattered at the bottom, fell over the tops of his black cowboy boots. His tan skin made her heart race. She stood up and wrapped her arms around him, and he pulled her close. Just as she leaned in for a kiss, Buck held up his finger and pressed it against her lips.

"Not now," Buck said. "It's time to get up."

"Get up?" Confused, she took a step back.

"It's time to get up," he repeated.

But this time, it wasn't Buck's voice, it was Matt's. She opened her eyes, but everything was blurry. When the room came into focus, there was Matt, standing over her.

"It's time to get up, sleepyhead," he said with a boyish smile. "It's almost ten."

Katie sat up and looked around. The dream had seemed so real. She really thought she was home, and now she just felt disoriented. Matt watched her and chuckled.

"You were totally out of it, weren't you?"

She ran her fingers through her auburn curls. "Yeah, I guess I was. That was some dream."

"Really?" he said. "What did you dream of?"

Katie looked out the window and then back at Matt. "Home," she said, smiling. "I dreamed of home."

"I know you're missing it, Kat, but I am really glad that you're here with me." He sat down on the edge of the bed and leaned toward her.

"Matt," Katie said as she covered her mouth, "if you kiss me right now, you will die. The dragon breath is real." She laid her head back on the pillow.

Matt laughed. "You take care of your dragon breath and I'll meet you downstairs when you're ready, okay?" He walked toward the door.

❧

Maggie sipped her hazelnut coffee and looked at Matt over the top of her blue-and-white mug.

"This is huge, Matty," she said, setting her cup down on the granite countertop.

"Are you absolutely sure you're absolutely sure?" Russell asked.

"I think he is, hon," Maggie said. "They've known each other for a long time."

Matt got up and sat next to his mom. He took her hand. "Mom," he said, grinning ear to ear. "I have never been so sure of anything in my life."

"Here," he said, reaching into the pocket of his khaki pants and pulling out a small, black box. "I'll show you just how sure I am."

"Sure of what, Matt?" Katie strolled into the kitchen, and he scrambled to shove the box back into his pocket.

Watching her move across the room wearing the cute, teal-blue summer dress that she and his mom had picked out at a boutique on Main Street made him even more sure of what he wanted to do. She was so beautiful, and he couldn't take his eyes off her. Her hair was pulled back in a cas-

94

cade of curls that fell just over the tops of her shoulders, and her burgundy red lips were screaming to be kissed.

"Sure of what?" she repeated, pouring herself a cup of coffee.

Russell jumped in. "Sure of how happy we are that you're here with us for this beautiful day of boating, that's what."

"I love boats!" Katie exclaimed. "I went out on the ocean once on a dolphin tour. The waters were so choppy, but we saw tons of dolphins, so it made up for the massive rockin'."

Matt breathed a sigh of relief. When Katie turned her back, Matt mouthed a thank you to his dad. Russell smiled and gave him a wink and a fist bump.

"This isn't just any boat though, babe," Matt said as he walked over to her. "This is a top-of-the-line sailboat."

"Top-of-the-line sailboat, huh? Does that mean I'll be getting top-of-the-line treatment, Matt?" She kissed his cheek and walked over to the table.

If only she knew how perfect this day will be for her, Matt thought. Katie looked over at Maggie and Russell. "Will you guys be joining us?" She took a sip of her coffee.

Maggie grinned. "Not for the boat ride itself, but we'll be there for dinner afterwards. Shall we eat breakfast on the deck this morning?"

The sun was warm on Katie's face as they stepped outside. The deck overlooked their neighbor's swimming pool, where a group of children were splashing and laughing and doing cannonballs into the water.

She smiled at Matt. "So, I know we have a boat ride and dinner planned for later, but what are we going to do this morning?"

Matt took her hand and kissed it. "Well, I have to run into work for a few, but you and my mom will be going to have a spa day."

Katie squealed with delight and tapped her toes on the maroon wood of the deck. "Aww, what about your dad, Matt? We can't leave him out."

"Don't you girls worry about me," Russell said. "I will find something to do."

Maggie winked at him. "You could always come with us and get a wax job."

"No thank you, dear. I believe I will have to pass on that one." He laughed.

Katie was having such a good time. She truly enjoyed being here, and she loved the people she was with. But as they sat and talked about the day ahead, Katie couldn't help but think of how much better it would be if Buck and her dad could join them. Buck would love the ocean, and her dad would love sitting out here on the deck watching the sunsets and sunrises.

"Well," Matt said, "I have to run, but I'll see you at the dock later, my lady." He bent down and kissed Katie goodbye and walked down the deck stairs to the cobblestone driveway.

She watched him drive out of sight. She was so torn. She loved Matt, she really did, but she had an ache in her heart for Buck. It was a true dilemma: California dreamin' or farm livin'? Fast cars or slow tractors?

Katie and Maggie spent hours at the spa. That morning, wearing a soft, white robe with her hair wrapped in a white towel, she truly felt like a princess. She had her fingernails done with an exquisite French tip and her toenails painted a burgundy red. Her stress melted away during a long massage with hot, scented oils.

During their facials, Katie sat up in her reclining chair and looked at Maggie, who was sitting next to her. "Could this get any better?"

Maggie smiled and sighed. "I think this is as good as it gets, girl. For me anyway," she said. "But for you ..." She chuckled.

Katie was curious about that chuckle. She wondered what that last remark meant, but before she could ask, they had to end the conversation to let the spa attendant apply the firming masks.

◈

Matt didn't really have to go into work today—he just needed some extra time at the dock to set up for their boat ride. On the small table in the middle of the boat, he set out a bottle of sweet red wine, which he knew was Katie's favorite. To go along with it, he'd brought a bowl of fruit and berries, which he placed in the minifridge.

Soft music played on the sailboat's speakers as he prepared everything. When he was done, he stepped back and snapped a few pictures, figuring the beginning of the rest of their lives deserved some good photos.

Time dragged on as he waited for his mom and Katie to arrive. Finally, he spotted them walking down the dock. He climbed out of the boat to greet them.

"Boy, oh boy," he said, "I didn't think you could get any lovelier, but here you are killing it."

"Why, thank you, Matty," his mom said. "I was hoping you would notice." She giggled and turned all the way around.

Katie also laughed. Man, her laughter was music to his ears.

"Yes, Mom," he said as he leaned in and kissed her cheek. "You look lovely, too."

Katie gave Maggie a hug and thanked her for a wonderful day at the spa.

"You're more than welcome. I'll see you guys at the restaurant tonight."

Matt nodded, said goodbye to his mom, then turned to Katie. "I couldn't wait to see you, Kat. This morning felt like an eternity."

Katie giggled and gave him a playful shove. "You goof. It's only been a few hours."

"Still ..."

"This is a beautiful boat, Matt," Katie said, looking it over before stepping on board. White on the outside with a glossy, hardwood finish inside, the sailboat was in impeccable condition. The rigging looked brand new.

"Nothing but the best for my girl," he said. "Amazingly enough, the salt water hasn't eaten away at everything."

"I must say, Matt, you've done very well for yourself." They boarded and set sail.

As they drifted further out onto the water, Katie took her phone out of her purse and snapped some pictures. Matt was glad she was enjoying herself.

"By the way, I have a surprise for you," Matt said, and went to grab the bowl of fruit and berries. On his way back, the boat rose sharply as it hit a rogue wave, then dropped back down. Matt staggered backward and reached out with his free hand to steady himself.

"Matt!" Katie set her phone down and stood up to offer her hand, but instead she fell right into him. As he tried to catch her, he let go of the bowl, and—*plink!*—it disappeared into the water.

Matt peered over the edge of the sailboat, then turned back around and laughed at his misfortune. "Well, at least we'll be extra hungry for our dinner tonight."

"And the fish will have a nice snack!" Katie said, sitting back down at the table. "What is it with you and water, Matt?" she said. "Back home, you fell into the water fountain, and here you almost fell into the ocean."

Matt looked at her, embarrassed but trying to smile. "What can I say, I'm just drawn to the water, I guess." He set about lowering the sail.

Seagulls passed overhead, cawing as they glided through the air. The salty sea air smelled like heaven, and he couldn't imagine being anywhere else but here in this moment. When he had finished lowering the sail, he grabbed the bottle of wine and sat down beside her.

"What do you think, Kat? Be honest."

"I love this Matt, I really do. It's so wonderful."

Matt rubbed her cheek softly with the back of his fingers. "And I love you." He leaned in to kiss her.

CHAPTER SIXTEEN

False Alarm

Randy couldn't wait to start building the vineyard on his farm. He and Buck had been toiling under the sweltering sun for hours to get the area ready for construction.

They took a break and surveyed what they'd done so far. The grass had been mowed, the equipment put away, the animals tended to.

Buck wiped his brow. "You're working me to the bone here, Randy."

Randy chuckled. "Well, son, a hard day's work equals a hard day's pay, right?"

Buck finished throwing feed to the chickens while Randy gathered tools to put back in the barn.

"Do you really think we can have a vineyard here, Boss?"

"I see it this way, Buck. If I don't at least try, I will never know. What I do know is that I have plenty of fertile ground for it. I found that out a while back when I had my soil analyzed."

Randy knew it would be a chore of staggering proportions, but also knew it could be done, provided they had what they needed. He'd hired some construction workers and worked out a deal with White's Winery to use their equipment to process his grapes in exchange for a portion of his profits. He wouldn't be able to do everything on his land, but he could certainly grow the grapes—and eventually, peaches.

"When are we going to start preparing the soil for the workers?" Buck asked.

"As soon as possible, I reckon," Randy said, walking out of the barn. "It's a Saturday, and those folks won't want to be out in the sun any more than we will."

"Okay. I'll get done what I can, and when they get here, they can take over, seeing as how I don't know the first thing about vineyards. I dunno, Randy. I'm still skeptical about all this. But good on you for going after what you want."

Randy chuckled and shook his head. He understood where Buck was coming from. Maybe it wouldn't work. Maybe he was having a midlife crisis, except instead of buying a Ferrari, he was planting a vineyard. But he

99

had to try. He wanted Katie to have something that would ensure she was taken care of after he was gone. Something special to honor both Katie and his late wife. This was it, and he was going to do everything in his power to make it a reality.

As the afternoon wore on, Randy was ready to call it a day. "What do you say to a tall glass of beer at Joe's and some wings, Buck?" They walked toward the house.

⊰

The arctic air hit Buck as soon as he opened the front door of the house.

"On a day like today," he said. "I'll go anywhere that has nice A/C like this."

"Agreed," Randy said, closing the door. "Well, I'm going to hit the shower. Why don't you clean up in Katie's room? I don't think she'll mind. That way we won't smell like sweaty garbagemen when we show up at Joe's."

"Deal, Boss," Buck said. He was filthy after unloading all the dirt the trucks had brought in earlier. He always kept an extra outfit in his pickup truck for just this situation, and he ran out to get it.

When he opened the door to Katie's room, the faint scent of her lilac perfume still lingered in the air. He breathed it in as deeply as he could. Before heading into the bathroom, he opened the door to her walk-in closet and took a peek. The scent was even stronger in there. *She must spray it on herself after she gets dressed in here*, Buck thought.

"Who's the creepy stalker now?" he scolded himself under his breath. He went into the bathroom to get cleaned up.

The warm water running down his body instantly perked him up. Squeezing some of Katie's lavender soap into his hands, he was suddenly back at the county fair with her, holding her as they watched the fireworks.

He snapped himself out of his trance and finished showering, then got dressed and headed downstairs, where Randy was already waiting for him.

It was unusually loud and crowded at Joe's Place, but they were still greeted by Joe himself, who shouted to them from across the diner. They found a booth by the window and ordered two tall glasses of beer and two plates of wings.

When his beer arrived, Buck took a long pull. "So, when do you think all this work will be finished, Randy?"

"At this point, it's hard to tell," Randy said, sitting up straight and taking of sip of his beer. "I know we made a big dent in it today, so I'm hoping that with all of us working on it, it won't be too long."

The waitress brought over their wings, and they dug in.

"You know, Randy, I was thinking—"

"Don't hurt yourself by doing that too much," Randy said, slapping the table and laughing.

"Ha, ha. Aren't you funny."

"Go ahead, Buck. I'm just messing with you. What were you going to say?"

"What I was going to say before I was rudely interrupted," he said, "was that I think ... I mean ... hmm." Buck didn't quite know how to put what he was going to say, and he wanted to make sure the words that left his lips were the right ones.

"I love your daughter, Boss. I want to take care of her and make sure she has everything she wants and everything she needs. The way I feel when she's around me is beyond words. I want to have that feeling every day."

He looked down at his hands and back up at Randy, then took a deep breath. "I guess what I'm saying is, well, I would like your blessing to ask for Katie's hand in marriage."

Buck was relieved to finally have that out of his system. He just didn't know how Randy would take it.

Randy pushed his plate to the side. "I know Katie feels for you in many of the same ways," he said. "I see how she looks at you when you're around, and I also know what she says to me when you're not."

Buck braced himself for what he knew Randy was about to say.

"Have you considered her feelings for Matt, though? I know it isn't something you want to hear, but we have to think of everything."

Randy was right, but he ached to have Katie by his side, and he wanted her there for all eternity.

101

Katie and Matt wrapped up their sailboat voyage with another glass of wine and talk of years past. As much as she was enjoying herself, however, Katie couldn't shake the dream she'd had about Buck. That made her feel terrible because Matt had put this whole day together for her, and here she was thinking about another man. But she'd have to make a decision soon. What was she going to do?

Do I dare rekindle my past love, or should I venture into new and uncharted territories with Buck? What happens if I blow off Matt, but it doesn't work out with Buck? And if I stay with Matt, will I always regret it and wonder what could've been with Buck? Her mind spun with different scenarios.

Clang, clang, clang! went the overhead bell as they pulled into the dock. Matt reached out and secured the boat with a heavy, tattered rope, looping it around and around the weathered support column of the dock. He climbed out of the boat and reached for Katie's hand to help her out.

As they walked arm in arm back to his truck, she couldn't help but bring up the fruit bowl incident on the boat. "I can't wait to tell your parents that story," she said, laughing.

They pulled up to the restaurant at a quarter after six. It was beautiful inside. The soft music and decorations on the walls set the mood and made it every bit as romantic as she thought an evening in a small village in Italy would be.

She had never been in a restaurant this nice. The chandeliers on the ceiling cast a dim glow on the tables, which were set with white tablecloths, red linen napkins, and shiny wine glasses. The food smelled delicious.

"This place must cost a fortune," Katie said, looking around.

"Nothing but the best for my girl." Matt put his hand on the small of her back and led her to their table, where Maggie and Russell were already seated and sipping red wine.

"Sorry to hold you up, guys," Matt said. He pulled out Katie's chair for her, then sat down and placed his napkin on his lap. "Traffic was terrible."

"How was your ride on the boat?" Russell asked, looking at Katie.

She laughed. "Oh, have I got a story to tell you!"

Matt smiled and rolled his eyes as Katie told them all about how he almost fell overboard. And she couldn't tell that story without also telling them about his tumble into the water fountain back home.

"What can I say," Matt said after she finished. "You make my knees weak when I'm with you."

Katie rubbed his cheek as she laughed. Their waitress came over to take their order, and after glancing at the menu she chose lasagna and garlic bread, along with an iced tea to drink.

After she ordered, Katie stood up. "If you will excuse me, I am going to head to the restroom." She looked at Matt. "Please don't go near any water while I'm gone." Matt's parents chuckled at that as she walked off.

Katie looked at herself in the mirror before she went back to the table. "So? What are you going to do?" she asked herself out loud.

Matt had waited all day to show his parents the ring he'd bought, so while Katie was away, he fished it out of his pocket and opened the box for them to see.

He had it all planned out. His dad had arranged for a guitarist to come to the table and play for them. Right after that, Matt would get down on one knee and ask Katie to marry him.

On her way back to the table, Katie saw Matt pull a small, black box out of his pocket and open it. His mom's reaction all but confirmed what it was.

He's actually going to propose! she thought. *What do I do now? Think! I can't go back in there because I don't know if I want to marry him or not. If he proposes and I say no, it will break his heart and embarrass him in front of the whole restaurant. If I say yes, well, I shudder to think.*

Frantic, she looked around for some means of escape, and that's when she saw it. *Oh no,* she thought. *No way. I'm not going to pull the fire alarm.*

Yet there it was, only a few feet away, calling to her. Would she be proud of herself for doing it? No. Would her dad be proud of her? No. Did she have any other choice right now? Also no.

Katie Calhoun, it's now or never, girl. Do it!

103

She hovered against the wall and took a few steps toward the alarm. Just as she reached her hand out, two patrons walked by, and she turned around to face them, smiling. As soon as they passed, she pulled the alarm. A shrill siren rang out across the restaurant, and bright strobe lights flashed on the walls and ceiling.

To add to the mayhem, the ceiling sprinklers came on, causing many of the women to jump up from their tables and hurry toward the exits, screaming and holding napkins over their heads to keep their hair dry.

From behind a partition just outside the dining area, Katie kept an eye on Matt and his parents, who were looking around in shock at the unfolding scene.

Through the chaos, she could hear Matt. "What? No!" he shouted. "This cannot be happening right now!"

He stood up and pointed toward the front entrance. "Mom and Dad, you go outside, and I'll look for Katie. Man, I will never live this down, especially since she just told me to stay away from water."

Russell grabbed several linens and held them over Maggie's head as he helped her out of the restaurant. Matt, already drenched from head to toe, split off and headed right toward Katie. She ducked behind the partition and made a beeline for the side door, hoping he didn't see her.

CHAPTER SEVENTEEN

Marriage Bliss... Goodbye Kiss

"So," Buck said, "if we find out that Katie doesn't feel for Matt what she feels for me, would you give me your blessing for Katie's hand then?"

Randy took a deep breath. "How about starting with a first date," he said, chuckling. "And maybe a second and third. Then we'll talk."

"Deal," he said as he reached across the table and shook Randy's hand. It wasn't exactly what he wanted to hear, but at least he wasn't being shown the door.

They paid for their food, said goodbye to Joe, and headed back to the farm. As they pulled up, a dark figure on the porch darted out of the shadows, in front of their headlights, and into the bushes. Buck reached down, heart pounding, and grabbed his gun from under his seat.

"There he is, Randy, that nutso stalker of Katie's!" he yelled. "Stop the car!" He had the door halfway open before Randy could even react.

As Buck flew out, Randy slammed on the brakes and put the car in park. He ran after Buck and caught up with him on the side of the house, just underneath Katie's bedroom window.

"I almost had him, Boss," Buck said, panting. "I almost had that guy!"

Randy rushed toward the front door. "I'm going to call Sergeant Haskins. They need to be out here A.S.A.P. He may have left a clue."

Not fifteen minutes later, Sergeant Haskins pulled his SUV into the driveway, followed by five squad cars with their lights flashing. He stepped out and walked up to the porch where Buck and Randy stood waiting. He shook their hands, then gave his officers orders to search the whole property, especially the barn.

"Let's go in and have a seat and you can tell me what happened," he said. They walked inside and sat in the living room, Buck and Randy on the couch and the sergeant in the recliner near the fireplace.

"Okay, gentlemen," he said as he opened his notepad. "Tell me what happened."

"As we pulled up to the house, we caught a glimpse of a man's profile before he took off like a bolt of lightning," Buck said, and told Sergeant Haskins the rest of the story.

"So you lost him when the bushes got too thick," Sergeant Haskins said, scribbling notes. "Can you describe what you saw in the headlights?"

Randy stood up. "I sure can. He was about five foot eleven or six foot, thin, dark-brown or maybe black hair. It doesn't surprise me at all that he could make it through that brush. Buck's not heavy by any means, but this fella was wiry."

An officer walked into the house carrying a photograph. "We found this out in the field, sir," he said, handing it to Sergeant Haskins.

Randy gasped when he saw it was one of their family photos. "I know this picture," he said. "It's the one I gave to Frank Merriman."

"Has this been logged as evidence already?" Sergeant Haskins asked his officer.

"Yes, sir."

Buck couldn't believe his eyes when Randy handed him the photograph. Black string had been wrapped around the picture. The only face visible was Katie's.

"Katie, I've been looking everywhere for you," Matt said as he ran outside and spotted her. "I even looked in the women's restroom."

He took her into his arms, and she gasped as the cold water soaked through her shirt and touched her skin.

"Sorry," he said. "Those stupid sprinklers would not stop."

A fire truck pulled into the parking lot and a crew of firefighters, in full gear, ran inside to inspect the building. Katie didn't mean to cause such a scene and was regretting that decision more and more. But she'd panicked and didn't know what else to do in that moment.

"I thought I told you to stay away from water, Matthew Fuller." She wanted to lighten the mood but only felt guilt.

Matt's dad walked up to them and rubbed Matt's shoulder. "How about we go home, son."

"Sounds good, Dad. That's enough excitement for one evening." Matt turned to Katie and opened the door for her to climb into the truck, then shut the door.

Matt stayed outside the truck to talk to his dad. He looked so upset. She had pulled the alarm so he wouldn't be hurt, but in the end, she had hurt him anyway. Perhaps better than humiliating him in front of his parents and the whole restaurant, but still, she had ruined his evening, and she felt horrible.

The ride back to Matt's was a silent one. When they got home, she went upstairs to put on her silk blue pajamas then back down to the kitchen to fix a cup of hot cocoa. She sat and thought of everything that had taken place that day: the relaxing morning at the spa with Maggie, the laughs they shared as they sailed on his gorgeous boat, and that beautiful restaurant.

I'll bet the food would've been delicious, she thought, knowing it was her fault none of them had been able to enjoy it. *Pulling the fire alarm? Really, Katie?*

But she was sure that deep down, there was a reason she'd resorted to such drastic measures and disrupted everyone's life at that restaurant today.

"You're the only girl I know who will drink hot cocoa on a hot summer's evening."

The voice startled her, and Katie spun around to see Maggie walking in. "I know it's weird, but it makes me think of home," she said, taking another sip.

"You're homesick, aren't you, Katie?"

She knew Maggie wasn't so much asking the question as just sympathizing with her. "More than you know," she said, taking a deep breath. "Today was wonderful, though. It was so relaxing being waited on hand and foot and being pampered like a queen."

"I would agree," Maggie said. "I keep telling Russell that's how I should be treated all the time. He doesn't seem to go for it, though." She chuckled, then leaned down and kissed Katie's forehead. "You get some rest, my dear. We love you."

Rest happened to be what she wanted most right now. On her way to her bedroom, Matt walked out of the bathroom with a towel around his waist. He had just showered, and he smelled so good.

Katie tousled his damp hair. "You just can't stay away from that dang water, can you?"

Before she could laugh, he took her hands in his. "I'm so sorry about tonight, Katie. That's not at all how I wanted it to end."

Yeah, she thought, *I might have had something to do with that.*

"Today was great, Matt. I really enjoyed it." Katie said in an attempt to cheer him up. She leaned in and kissed him.

She felt certain she'd made up her mind. "Always know that I love you and your family for caring for me and protecting me."

"Katie, come outside with me after I get dressed."

"Matt, I'm so—"

"Please?"

They went outside and sat on the deck, where a warm breeze greeted them. Matt turned off the lights so they could get a better view of the stars.

"Look, Katie ..."

She froze. *Oh no, is he going to propose here and now? I should have gone to bed. Just breathe,* she told herself. "Yes, Matt?"

"Whatever happened tonight happened, and I can't change it. I just want you to know I'm ready to finish what we started all those years back. That is, whenever you are."

He was so sincere. Hearing those heartfelt words made her feel like a terrible human being. She took a deep breath. "I know, Matt, and a part of me is, too, but there's so much going on back home right now. I can't just up and leave Dad on the farm, and ..."

"And what?" he said. "And Buck?" He stood up.

"Matt ..." She reached her hand out for him, and he pushed it away.

"Don't, Katie. Just don't," he said. "Don't bother, because it will only hurt us more." He walked off and slammed the door on his way in.

Matt burst into his room and threw himself on the bed. He was so jealous of Buck he couldn't stand it. He couldn't dream of another man touching her, kissing her, just being close to her in that way. That's why he wanted to marry her. He wanted to have her for always. That's how it would have ended had they not moved out to California. They would be married by now, and he wouldn't have to worry about another man capturing her heart.

❧

Katie stayed outside, gazing up at the stars and confused as ever about what had just happened. But she couldn't be mad at Matt.

"What I am doing is unfair to him," Katie said out loud. "I feel like I'm leading him on, and in a way, I guess I am. That's not my intention, but I just enjoy our time together. I don't want to marry Matt until I know what there is or isn't with Buck." Tears welled up in her eyes and she wiped them away.

"Oh, Momma, I am in such a pickle. What am I going to do?" Katie searched the midnight sky for some kind of answer.

The wind swept across her face and a strand of hair rubbed against her cheek. Katie brushed it out of the way, and a smile spread across her face.

"I have to be true to myself before I can be true to others," she said, standing up. She went back inside and tiptoed up the stairs.

The muffled sound of a song they had danced to years ago came from Matt's room. She stopped in front of his closed door, took a deep breath, then went to her room.

She lay in bed for a long time, staring out at the flickering street-light, weighing her options. The words "Stay true to yourself" kept ringing in her ears.

What is it I want? Katie thought. *I, I, I. Is it only about me?* She knew she wasn't a selfish person, but sometimes felt like she was only considering herself. *And who will it hurt if I'm wrong?* Finally, at one o'clock in the morning, she knew what she had to do.

She got out of bed and put on some clothes, then crept outside her room to make sure everyone was asleep. The house was dark except for the night lights illuminating the hallway. The light was off in Matt's room, and she could hear Russell snoring down at the end of the hallway.

Back in her own room, she packed her suitcase. Then, sitting down to look at herself in the mirror, she took a deep breath.

"Katie," she told herself, "it's now or never."

CHAPTER EIGHTEEN

Raining on My Heart

Buck sat down next to Randy, who was visibly shaken by the photo the police had found. He placed his hand on Randy's shoulder.

"It just ain't right, Buck," Randy said, wringing his hands. "How could he have gotten that picture? That was Frank's. I saw it myself in Frank's office."

"Do you think our stalker could be Frank?" Buck asked.

Randy stood up and paced across the living room floor. "Couldn't be, Buck. He wouldn't do something like this."

But did he know that for sure? In all the confusion, nothing seemed certain. Sergeant Haskins and his team had stationed themselves outside for the rest of the night, not just in the driveway, but in the barn and vineyard as well.

"It's just precautionary, guys," Sergeant Haskins had told them.

Even with the extra security, Randy wasn't sure that he would be able to sleep at this point. Buck didn't seem too tired, either. They both had so much adrenaline coursing through their veins, they probably could have taken down a grizzly bear with their bare hands. In his mind, Randy replayed every conversation he'd had with Frank lately, and asked Buck to do the same.

"I remember telling him Katie was leaving town," Buck said. "So why would Frank be here knowing she's not?"

"How, why, what, when?" he said, still pacing. "How, why, what, and when?"

"Come on, Boss, don't flip out on me. You're sounding like a crazy man."

"No really, these are the questions going through my mind." He stopped and turned to face Buck. "How, as in, how did whoever this is get that picture? Why does he have it, and what does he want with Katie? Finally, when did he get his hands on this picture? Once we have the answers to these questions, I believe we'll have our stalker." He sat back down on the couch and looked over at Buck.

111

❧

That was close, Tate said to himself as he scrambled up a hill and took refuge behind a tree. Now, all I need is to see her face. Then I'll feel better. He reached into his jacket pocket for the photo, but it wasn't there.

His heart raced. He stood up, careful not to show the slightest sign of movement, even though the house had been quiet for some time. He searched every pocket of his pants and turned his jacket inside out. Nothing.

"Dammit," he whispered. "I must have dropped it." But where? He sat down and put his head in his hands. It was getting harder and harder to see her at all. He never saw her at the grocery store anymore, and her bedroom curtains were always closed. The only time he could catch a glimpse was if her dad and that baboon guy friend of hers happened to allow her to go outside. Now I can't even see her face in a picture, he thought. He sighed and shook his head. What will I do now?

❧

"Well," Buck said, with determination in his voice and a gleam in his eyes, "I reckon our first stop in the morning will be to talk to Frank and see what he has to say about this."

Randy sighed. He was tired, so tired, of this nonsense, and he missed his girl. He wanted Katie home so badly. It would be different if she had simply moved to her own place. But this ... this was ridiculous. She had to travel out of town just for her safety.

"What happened to the good old days, Buck, when you could go outside and have a good time and not worry about fools pulling stuff like this?" Randy stood up. "It's really late, buddy. We should get some sleep." He walked toward the stairs.

❧

Buck felt so bad for Randy. Katie was his lifeline, and he could see the hurt in his eyes. He wanted to right this wrong, to make them all feel safe again. But above all, he wanted Katie back home. The scent of her perfume was fading throughout the house. All the flowers she had brought home had wilted, and her tea pitcher had been emptied, washed, and put away long ago. Buck went outside to sit in Katie's rocking chair and look at the sky. He took comfort in thinking that maybe, just maybe, they were making a wish upon the same star.

❧

Katie crept out of her room and rolled her suitcase down the hall. She had called the local cab company to drive her to the airport. Even though she felt bad about leaving this way, she knew in her heart it was for the best. She could only hope Matt would understand that.

The taxi driver lifted her bags into the trunk, and they drove off. Light rain fell and the streets had turned a glossy black. The streetlights overhead reflected off the windows in a wet blur. She couldn't contain her excitement about seeing her dad, her home, and Buck. A feeling of comfort swept over her, just imagining herself in his arms, face to face with him, nose to nose, heart to heart. Feeling his breath on her neck, his lips upon hers ...

"Miss?" The taxi driver's voice snapped her out of her daydream. "We're here, miss. Do you need help with your luggage?"

Katie smiled at him. "No thank you, sir. I can manage," she said, handing him the fare. "Here you go. Keep the change and have a safe night."

She stood outside the airport for a few moments. Then she took a deep breath and walked up to the glass doors, which slid open to let her in.

❧

A bad dream jarred Matt out of his slumber. He got out of bed and walked to the bathroom to splash water on his face. Back in his room, he looked at the time. *Four o'clock. Still early.*

113

He climbed back into bed but couldn't fall asleep. All he could think about was how they'd left each other last night. She was hurting and he was angry, frustrated, jealous. Maybe he had reacted the wrong way. Maybe he should have taken her hand and proposed to her right then and there.

"I wasn't fair to her," he said to himself. "I should have taken her feelings into consideration. I can't believe what an idiot I am."

He so badly wanted to wake Katie up but thought better of it. Even though she was always able to make him feel better when he was upset, it was a selfish reason to wake her so early, and he'd been selfish enough already.

But he had to see her. He tossed back his dark-blue duvet, climbed out of his warm bed, and threw on his bathrobe.

As he opened his door, the soft scent of lilacs hit him and went straight to his head. He glanced down the dimly lit hallway. The only sound was muffled snoring coming from his parents' room.

He tapped on Katie's door, then opened it a crack.

"Kat," he whispered, pushing the door open.

The room was pitch dark, which he found strange. Usually when he came in to wake her in the mornings, the curtains were open. She loved to lie in bed and watch the midnight sky and see the stars dancing in the light of the moon. Why did she close them tonight?

"Kat?" he whispered again, fumbling for the lamp. He switched it on. "Are you—"

What the ...? The bed was made, and Katie was nowhere to be seen.

He hurried to the bathroom, thinking that she could have fallen or gotten hurt. If so, he wouldn't have heard a thing over the music he'd been playing earlier. He turned on the light in the bathroom. She wasn't there, and neither was her makeup bag that she kept next to the sink. Pushing back the shower curtain, he saw that her small bottles of bath wash and shampoo were also gone. He was so confused. Where could she be? He ran downstairs to check the kitchen, the living room, the deck. Nothing. He charged back up and banged on the door to his parents' room.

"Mom, Dad, wake up!" Matt said, opening the door.

"Matty? What ..." Maggie clicked on her bedside lamp.

Russell sat up. "What time is it? What the heck is going on?" he asked, squinting.

"She's gone," Matt said. "Kat isn't here. She isn't anywhere. All her stuff is gone. She just disappeared." Tears filled his eyes.

114

His mom threw her covers off and slipped her robe on over her pajamas. She followed Matt to Katie's room to see for herself.

"Did you already try calling or texting her?" she asked, glancing around the empty room.

"Yeah. Straight to voicemail."

"I'll call Randy in a couple of hours. If you ask me, that's where she's headed. She's gotten herself onto a plane and taken off for home," Maggie said. "But there's no sense in calling him so early in the morning and getting him all upset. If that's where she's going, she has a long flight ahead of her."

"Did Katie say anything about leaving or not wanting to be here anymore?" Matt asked his mom.

Maggie sat down on the bed and took a deep breath. "No, nothing like that. I talked to her last night and all she said was she was feeling homesick."

Matt lowered his head and sighed. "This is all my fault that she's gone."

Maggie looked up at him. "Your fault? How is it your fault?"

"Well, last night, we ..." He sat down next to her and told her about their argument.

"Love is a mighty tricky thing, son," she said. "You can't force yourself on someone and make them love you. There's no doubt in my mind that she loves you, Matt, but is she still *in* love with you? That's the question you have to ask yourself. Just be prepared to get an honest answer." She kissed her thumb and placed it on his forehead as she stood up. She used to do that when he was a young boy, and it always made him feel happy.

"I'm going to make some coffee, Peanut. Come down if you want some."

As she walked out, he caught sight of a piece of paper sticking out from underneath the nightstand. He reached down and picked it up. His name was written on it.

To Matt

His hands trembled as he unfolded it. Taking a deep breath, he began reading what Katie had written, dreading every word.

❧

Before she knew it, Katie was boarding her flight. Soon, she would be home. The thought of that made her smile but also brought butterflies to her stomach. She pulled out her phone to text her dad, but then decided against it, wanting to make it a surprise instead.

Sitting back in her seat next to the window, she smiled and watched the rain splashing the glimmering asphalt of the tarmac.

"Let's go home," she said to herself. "Let's go home."

❧

My dearest Matt,

I know that as you read this, you will have blamed yourself for my leaving. Let me first say that it was not your fault. You helped me see something that I needed to see, but the argument we had last night under the stars isn't my reason for leaving. I can't thank you or your parents enough for taking me in and making sure I was taken care of. I will treasure you guys and your love forever. But I was doing you an injustice by being there. I felt I was leading you on and that's not fair to either one of us.

Matt, you would stop the world and place it in my hand if I asked you to. But I am not sure I'm at the same point you are anymore. In the past, I would've done that without hesitation. But we have to be honest here. We can't live in the past anymore. I love you, Matthew Fuller, with my whole heart. But I have to go back home. I need to be with my dad. He needs me, too. The ache in your heart can't be soothed, I know, and I am sorry for the pain I'm causing you. I will remember everything we did while we were all together, especially our sailing trip.

You have an amazing heart. Please stay true to it. Now, I must stay true to mine. Kiss your mom and dad for me and tell them I'm sorry I left without telling them goodbye. I just couldn't bear to look you in the eyes and walk away.

I love you,

Katie

He held the letter to his chest and cried. But he knew the words she wrote were true. His mom's question swirled around in his head. *She loves me, but is she* in *love with me?* From the note she'd written, it didn't seem like it. That was the honest answer he needed.

Holding the letter in his fingertips, he shuffled downstairs, where his mom and dad were seated at the kitchen table. He set the piece of paper in front of them.

"Read it," he said. "She's gone. Flat gone. In every sense of the word. She went back home."

Russell put on his reading glasses, picked up the letter, and read it out loud.

"Well, son," he said, taking off his glasses and setting the letter back on the table. "I know this isn't easy for you, and I know you love her, but she has to do what's best for her. At least now, with this letter, you know what she was thinking."

Maggie reached across the table and placed her hand over his. "We'll get through this, Matty," she said. "You can call her later this evening to see how she is." The smile she gave him was weak, but it still brought him comfort.

The truth was, he'd already texted her several times but hadn't heard back. He so badly wanted to keep sending messages until she responded, but he knew if he did that, he wouldn't be any different than this whack job who had been following her.

CHAPTER NINETEEN

Welcome Home… Maybe?

Katie asked for a pillow from the flight attendant walking past her seat. She was a little nervous. It was only her second time on a plane, and this time, she was alone. Sitting near a window helped, though.

God sure does paint a pretty picture, she thought, taking in the view. Outside, the hues of blue and purple that mingled with wisps of pink and white helped her relax.

Katie leaned her head back against the pillow and closed her eyes. Soon, she was fast asleep, dreaming of the moment she arrived back home. After being away for so long, happiness finally filled her heart.

A pocket of turbulence shook her awake. For the next several minutes, the dipping and rocking only got worse, and she tightened her grip on her armrest. Her heart raced, and she suddenly felt afraid and very alone.

"Are you okay, honey? You look terrified." It was the same flight attendant who had brought her the pillow.

"I don't fly much, and I guess I'm not used to turbulence like this."

"It'll be okay, honey," she said. "It's just an air pocket. Nothing to worry about. Tell you what, I have a few extra magazines and books in my bag. Would you like something to read?"

"That would be great," Katie said, smiling and breathing in her scent. "Thank you."

Katie loved to read and had been an avid reader since she learned how. At one point, she'd even started to write a novel, but had only written a few chapters before the fire at the farm upended her life.

"Take whatever you'd like, honey," the flight attendant said, holding out an assortment of reading material for Katie to choose from.

As she leaned toward her, Katie picked up the scent of Sea Island cotton, and it transported her back to her childhood, when the dryer sheets her mom used would fill the house with the sweet smell of cotton every time she did laundry.

A novel by Nicholas Sparks caught Katie's eye. He was one of her favorite authors, and she knew a love story would soothe her rattled nerves. She settled in to read it.

119

Randy woke up early and opened the front door to grab the morning newspaper. As he brewed a pot of coffee and poured himself a cup, he thought of how much he missed having Katie around to greet him in the mornings.

He had just sat down at the table and opened the paper when the doorbell rang. It was Buck.

"Good morning, son!" Randy said, opening the front door. "I was just reading the paper. Fix yourself a cup of coffee and join me." As he sat down, he grabbed one of the chairs and pulled it out for Buck.

Buck brought his mug of coffee to the table, sat down, and took a sip. Randy set down his newspaper and looked him over. He had bags under his eyes and looked beat. He knew this was taking its toll on Buck, too, and he wanted to cheer him up.

"I had a great idea this morning," Randy said.

Buck glanced up from his cup. "Oh yeah? What's that?"

"Well, as you and I both know, we haven't seen Katie in over a month. I miss her terribly, and I know you do, too. So let's surprise her. Let's go to California!"

"Wow, Randy. I know you don't like long trips so I didn't think you'd be up for something like that. Are you serious?"

"Absolutely. Why not?"

"Do you think it would be weird if I came along? It's one thing for you to go since you're her dad, but as for me ... well, let's just say I'm not exactly Matt's favorite person."

Randy thought about that, then got up and walked over to the stove to prepare breakfast. "Well," he said, turning the burner on, "I think it would be fine. I can arrange for someone to look after the place for a couple of days. It'll be fun. We'll make an adventure out of it." Randy took some eggs and sausage out of the refrigerator and set them on the counter.

"It would be so great to see Katie's face and hear her voice in person instead of over a video call," Buck said. "And I'd love to give her a big hug."

Randy looked over at Buck, who was sitting at the table with a big smile on his face. He'd seemed down lately, so maybe this was just the kick in the pants Buck needed to feel happy and hopeful again.

As Randy cooked breakfast, they talked of their trip. They agreed it would be a great way not only to see Katie, but also to get away from this mess for a few days. A vacation.

"Well, I'm starting to think this is actually a great idea," Buck said so loudly it made Randy chuckle. "You should've had this idea a while ago!"

"I agree, son," Randy said. "But let's take care of some business first. I tossed and turned all night thinking of the possibility of Frank being involved in this." He sprinkled salt over the eggs as they sizzled in the pan.

"Yeah, I didn't sleep too well either," Buck said, downing the last of his coffee. "I just don't think he would be able to do that and then be able to look us in the face and be so cordial. I mean, I know that happens with psychopaths, but Frank just doesn't strike me as one."

"For what it's worth, I don't think he is, either." Randy walked to the table with two plates of food and set one in front of Buck. Then he sat down and said a blessing over his food before digging in.

After breakfast, they walked out into the hot summer sun and over to the vineyard that was nearing completion. Buck turned to Randy with a look of amazement on his face.

"What, boy?" Randy laughed. "Why are you looking at me like that?"

"It's just that ..." Buck stared straight ahead at the workers who were putting finishing touches on some of the details of the new vineyard. "Okay, I'll just say it. I never thought you'd be able to pull this off, Randy. But you really proved me wrong. I mean, look at it. It's gorgeous!"

Randy smiled. "Can I tell you a secret?" he said, leaning closer to Buck. "I didn't think I could pull it off, either."

It was a magnificent view, if he did say so himself. The freshly painted red barn, the corral they'd just built, green fields as far as the eye could see, and rows of grapes just waiting to grow and become wine all combined into a scene worthy of a painting.

"Katie will be floored when she sees what you've been up to all this time," Buck said, placing his hand on Randy's shoulder.

"Yeah, she will. But as much as I could stare out at this view all day, we really need to go talk to Frank."

❧

Katie stepped off the plane and took a deep breath of fresh air. She didn't realize how different the air was out in California. The air out there was somehow thicker, or maybe just not as fresh, as the air here.

As she stood at baggage claim waiting for her suitcase, a woman glanced over at her.

"It looks like someone's happy to be here," she said.

"Yes, I am," Katie replied. "How could you tell?"

"You're glowing, sweetie."

Katie believed it. She could feel her own eyes twinkling, and she couldn't keep her smile hidden.

"I'm finally home," Katie told her.

"Well then, welcome home."

"Thank you," Katie said, grabbing her suitcase off the carousel. She walked out the door and over to the taxi stand.

She didn't have to wait at all. Cabs were pulling up left and right, and she caught the next one in line. The driver looked younger than she expected and was very sweet. He helped her with her bags, then opened her door as she climbed into the back seat.

"Where will it be, miss?" he asked.

"Do you know where Merriman's Fresh Market is in Orange Grove?"

"That I do," the cabbie said. "I'm actually from Orange Grove, and Frank is a good friend of my family's."

Everything was falling neatly into place, like pieces of a giant puzzle. On the plane, Katie had second-guessed herself, thinking she'd made the wrong move or acted too hastily. But now she was convinced she'd made the right decision.

They pulled into the parking lot of Merriman's Fresh Market. She paid the taxi driver then walked into the store, luggage in tow.

Frank's face lit up when he saw her. He mouthed the words, "Oh my gosh!" as he came out from behind the customer service counter and trotted over to her.

"Katie Calhoun, you are a sight for sore eyes," he said, holding his arms out. "I have missed seeing you so much!" He wrapped his arms around her.

Katie laughed, hugging him back. "Why, thank you, it's good to see your face as well." She took a deep breath and caught the aroma of blueberry muffins and coffee. "That smell is to die for, Frank. I must have a cup of your famous coffee!"

"You got it, cupcake. On the house. Why don't you leave your bags over there? I'll make sure no one messes with them."

"Good idea, Frank." She rolled her luggage into the corner near the front door, then dropped her phone into the pouch of her suitcase and zipped it shut.

"By the way, Katie, you should go check out our flowers. Violet's here today, and she's got some real beauties. Fresh as can be!" He walked away to fetch Katie a cup of coffee.

Tate was stocking shelves with canned fruit when he heard Katie's name. His heart raced. Katie? Maybe he'd misheard. But then her sweet voice drifted over to him, and he knew for sure she was here. In the flesh.

He had to see her. Moving to the end of the aisle, he peeked around the corner while pretending to straighten the shelves so as not to be too obvious. Where was she? He craned his neck. Just then, she appeared, walking straight toward him. He ducked back into the aisle. It is her! he thought. Finally, she's back! She didn't notice him as she walked by, so he stepped out of the aisle and followed her from a distance. Her dark-blue jeans hugged every curve she had. Her white, button-up blouse flowed away from her body as she walked. His palms were sweaty, his breath shaky. "I've been waiting for you for too long, my love," he whispered. As she walked up to the flower stand and said hello to Violet, he crouched behind a shelf nearby.

"Hey, Violet," Katie said, walking up to the counter. Violet was looking down at an arrangement she was putting together.

When she looked up, her eyes widened, and she beamed. "Well, look what the cat dragged in! It's felt so empty here without you, and we have all these beautiful flowers in need of a home," she said, motioning

123

toward a rack filled with the new arrivals.

"And believe you me," Katie said, "I am sure our home is in need of them, too."

Violet laughed. "Yeah, I haven't seen your dad in here for at least a few days. And he never comes over here."

Katie walked over and smelled all the flowers, wanting to pick the very best ones for their house. She was going to be surprising them, after all.

"I'll take these right here," Katie said, setting some daisies and carnations on the counter. "Do me a favor, Violet. If you happen to see my dad today, don't let him know you saw me. I came home early to surprise them!"

Frank walked up and handed Katie a cup of coffee and a blueberry muffin. "There ya go, Katie," he said. "Brewed fresh just for you, and a sweet treat to go along with it."

She blew on the coffee to cool it down, then took a sip. "This hits the spot, Frank. And hazelnut, my favorite. Thank you so much."

"Well, I'm going to head back to my office," Frank said. "Be safe and come back soon."

"Oh, Frank?" Katie said. "Please don't let my dad know I'm home. I want to surprise him and Buck. They aren't expecting me." She smiled.

"You got it!" He turned and walked back toward his office.

Now's my chance, Tate thought. If no one knows she's here, then no one will know she's gone, either. And no one will miss her. This is it, Tate! Your big break!

"Shoot, I can't find it," Violet said, digging through a bin behind the counter.

"Find what?" Katie said. She took a bite of her muffin.

"The violet ribbon I always wrap your flowers with," she said, con-

124

tinuing to search. "I usually have so much of it on hand because I've made that my trademark. You know, my name being Violet and all. I know I had a roll here, but I can't find it for the life of me." She looked up. "Would you mind waiting here while I go to the back and grab some more?"

Katie set her cup down on the counter. "Violet, you don't have to go to the trouble. It's okay if you use a different ribbon."

"Don't be silly. I haven't been able to wrap flowers for you in a long time. It's no trouble at all."

As Violet walked away, Katie's eye was drawn to a book sitting on the counter with full-color pictures of floral arrangements. She took another sip of her coffee and flipped through the book.

You've been waiting long enough for this, he thought. Now is not the time to get nervous and chicken out.

He peered around one of the shelves and watched as she stood there looking through the book she had found on the counter. He crept up behind her, being careful not to make a sound. His heart pounded, and a single drop of sweat ran down from his dark hair onto his nose. He was close enough now that he could smell her perfume. Sweet and refreshing, just like her. Tate knew it was time. He seized the opportunity.

In the blink of an eye, he was on her. He wrapped his arms around her and placed a hand over her mouth so she couldn't yell for help or utter a cry of surprise.

"Don't make a sound, pretty lady," he whispered into her ear. "I have been waiting for you, and for this moment, for a long time. Don't make me have to hurt your beautiful face."

When Violet returned to the counter, Katie wasn't there. She figured she must have gone to do some shopping in the store. But it was odd that she would have left her coffee and half-eaten muffin on the counter, given how neat and tidy she was. Violet continued wrapping up Katie's arrangement, knowing she'd be back soon to pick it up.

Frank walked up to the counter. "Hey, Violet," he said. "Where's Katie? I forgot to tell her something when she came in."

Violet took a deep breath. "I'm not sure where she went, Frank. I went to grab some ribbon, and when I came back, her coffee and muffin were here, but she wasn't."

Frank rubbed his chin. "That's odd. Well, when she comes back, tell her to come find me. I have something to tell her." He tapped his hand on the counter and walked away.

❧

"It's pointless to scream," Tate said as he forced Katie through the employees-only entrance at the back of the store. "No one will hear you now."

She tried to bite his hand, but his grasp was too strong. All she wanted was to see her attacker, see his face. Was he dragging her out back to kill her? Suddenly she was terrified that she would never see her dad again. Or Buck. Or anyone.

I should have stayed in California, she thought.

A wave of nausea engulfed her, and she knew the muffin and coffee wouldn't stay down for long. *Stay calm, Katie, just stay calm. If you throw up or freak out, he'll kill you.*

She had watched enough true crime shows to know what to do and what not to do in situations like this. Katie took deep breaths through her nose as they walked. None of her surroundings were familiar anymore. She had never been around the back of the store. Tate tightened his grip as she slowed.

"Move!" he screamed. "I don't have time for you to lollygag around. They've probably already noticed you're gone. Faster!"

Twigs snapped underneath her feet as she picked up her pace.

Warm tears spilled from her eyes and dropped onto Tate's hand, causing him to loosen his grip. "Please don't hurt me," Katie gasped between breaths. "I'll do whatever you want, just please don't hurt me."

"Oh, don't you worry, my love," Tate said. "No harm will come to you. That is, as long as there's no funny business."

126

She moved faster to keep pace with him. As they started up a hill, her thighs burned with every step they took. She struggled to catch her breath.

"We're nearly there," Tate answered, also out of breath. "Nearly home."

CHAPTER TWENTY

Cave of Secrets

Out on the deck, Maggie dialed Randy's number and took a sip of coffee as she waited for him to pick up.

"No answer," she said to Matt, setting the phone down on the glass table beside her. "But let's try again in a little bit. They may be out in the fields or tending to the animals."

Matt sighed. "I don't know what to think now. How am I supposed to feel? Do I just let her go?" His mind was spinning out of control.

Maggie reached over to his chair and laid her hand on his. "You give her the time she needs, Matty. Right now, that's about all you can do."

❧

Randy and Buck pulled into the parking lot of Merriman's Fresh Market. They'd chatted the whole way over about the idea of traveling to see Katie. Buck could already see her beautiful face in his mind. He imagined taking her in his arms, holding her close, kissing her. His first instinct would have been to get her a big bouquet of flowers when they arrived, but he thought better of it. Giving her flowers that she would have to keep at another guy's house—a guy who was also in love with her—was probably in poor taste. He had to be a gentleman to everyone, Matt included.

"Are you ready, Buck?" Randy brought him out of his daydream and to the task at hand: settling this matter of the photo they'd found, and Frank's possible involvement.

❧

Frank was standing at the customer service counter when Randy and Buck

129

walked in. He was staring straight at them yet seeing right through them. His mind was spinning around in circles, confused as to where Katie would have gone. Her luggage was still there by the door, Violet had yet to see her, and she wasn't anywhere that either of them had checked. After a few moments, his mind registered Buck and Randy's presence.

"Hey, guys! How are you?" Frank said, walking over to them. He noticed the strained expressions on their faces. "What's the matter, fellas?"

"We need to have a serious talk, Frank," Randy said.

Frank was taken aback by Randy's tone. "Sure, of course," he said. "Uh, let's ... I guess we'll just go to my office, guys." He motioned for them to walk ahead of him.

Frank took a seat at his desk, and Randy and Buck sat in the chairs across from him.

Randy took a deep breath and began. "I'm not really sure how to say this, Frank, but ..."

Now Frank was even more concerned. What the heck did they need to talk to him about?

"You know how we've been having issues at our home," Randy continued. "Well, it's recently gotten worse." He went on to tell Frank about how they'd returned home last night to find a man sprinting off the porch, and about the picture the cops had found when they searched the property.

"The thing is, Frank, the only person I know of that had that picture was you."

Buck chimed in. "Care to explain?"

Frank sat back in his chair and put his hands up. "Fellas, take it easy. You can't seriously think that was me?" Frank asked, sounding confused and a little hurt at the same time. "Look, I have known you and your family forever, Randy. I would never do anything to harm you and Katie. You guys are like family to me."

Randy leaned forward. "I'm not trying to accuse you of anything, Frank, but I had to come here and clear the air. Please don't take this personally. I'm only trying to follow leads in what we've found, and this picture led us directly to you."

"Of course," Frank said. "I understand. That picture was here in my office, pinned to the corkboard. Besides me, the only people who have access to this office are my employees. Do you have a description of this stalker?"

"Yes," Buck said. "I have his exact description in my phone. Why do you ask?"

130

"Well, this is a small store, and I don't have that many employees, but what we could do is go through our personnel files and see if anyone matches your description." He stood up and walked over to his file cabinet.

"Dang," Buck said, patting his pocket. "I must have left my phone in the truck. Let me run and get it."

∽

Buck ran outside and grabbed his phone from the truck. As he walked back in, Katie's scent hit him as soon as the door opened. He stopped in his tracks and looked around, hoping to see her, but immediately chastised himself. Of course she wasn't here. He remembered the time he thought she was standing in his kitchen, only to turn around and see nothing.

But as he glanced back, he saw it: her luggage, sitting next to the door. His heart raced.

Was this here when we first walked in? he thought. *Were we just so distracted that we walked right past it?*

He grabbed the luggage and ran with it to Frank's office. Out of breath, he went through the door.

"Randy," Buck said, gasping, "Katie's home! I mean, Katie's here! This is her luggage."

Randy looked at Frank, eyes wide. "You knew she was here and didn't say anything? Why is she here? Is Matt with her?"

"I can explain," Frank said as he stood back up. "She came here alone, not all that long ago, and said she wanted to surprise you guys. She asked me not to say anything. Then, just before y'all got here, she left, and I was trying to figure out where she had gone to. There wasn't anyone with her, and she didn't mention anyone, either."

"What do you mean, trying to figure out where she had gone?" Randy said.

"Well, she came in and greeted me, and I told her to go see Violet because we'd just gotten some of her favorite flowers in. I brought her a cup of coffee and a blueberry muffin while she was talking to Violet. A few minutes later, I came back to the flower stand and she was gone."

"So, where did she go?" Buck asked, growing irritated.

"We looked around the whole store right before you got

131

here, guys."

Randy stood up. "Given what's been going on at home, she could be in grave danger right now," he said, looking at Frank and Buck.

Frank stood up, too. "I had no idea all this was going on, guys. If I had, I would have stopped her or stayed with her or something." He shook his head. "I'm sorry, guys. This is all my fault."

"Now isn't the time to start placing blame," Buck said. "If you didn't know, you didn't know. The main thing now is finding her and making sure she's okay."

"Buck's right," he said. "Frank, are there cameras in the store that might have caught what happened? Maybe she had an inkling we were coming and decided to hide somewhere. That's where video footage would really help."

At the top of the hill, Tate stopped in front of the dark entrance to a cave. From behind her, he yanked on her hands. Katie winced in pain.

"We're home, Princess!" Tate said in a sing-songy voice.

Katie looked around, panting. *Home?* she thought. *This is a cave on top of a hill. How could this be home?*

Tate gave her a shove. "Go into the cave, Katie."

She stumbled forward and trembled. The entrance looked deep, and she was afraid that if she went in, she wouldn't come back out. All she wanted right now was to be home in the comfort of her dad's arms.

Spider webs coated the walls of the entrance passage. As he forced her further into the cave, the light of the sun faded, and by the time the passage opened up into a larger room, she could see almost nothing.

"Have a seat," Tate said, releasing her hands and motioning to the ground. "Make yourself at home."

She knelt on the cold, dusty floor of the cave while Tate walked around lighting candles that sat on small rock ledges. Katie couldn't wait to see his face and find out who had kidnapped her.

This whole time, she'd only heard his voice and felt his hot, sweaty breath on her neck. She strained her eyes and tried hard to make out any of his features, but it was just too dark.

132

After he had lit all the candles, she saw that each candle sat inside a ring of leaves. In the center of the room, she could make out a crude firepit with sticks and piles of ash inside.

Drat, I still can't see him, she thought. *Maybe he will start a fire soon and I'll be able to figure out who this guy is. Then I'll finally know who it was that kept me captive in my own home, kept me from going out at night to look at the stars, kept me from opening my curtains, and kept me feeling so unsafe I had to leave town.*

Tate disappeared behind what she thought was a small wall, or possibly another room. If there were ever a time to escape, it was now. He didn't have her hands tied, obviously trusting she would stay put. Katie looked around, trying to find the quickest way out.

"You want some water?" came Tate's voice from the darkness.

"Um, sure?" Katie answered as she scooted closer to the entrance passage.

But just as she was ready to bolt, he came back into the room, skirted around her, and crawled out toward the entrance to the cave, where for a fleeting moment, the light of the sun caught him.

Finally, a face. She looked at him so hard she was sure he could feel her dumbfounded stare piercing his soul.

Tate Stevens?

CHAPTER TWENTY-ONE

Without a Trace

They all walked back to the security office to review what the cameras in the store had captured that day.

Frank pulled up a chair in front of the computer while Randy and Buck stood behind him. "Here's the footage from earlier, guys," Frank said. "Let's see what's on here."

The images that appeared on the screen were grainy, the video choppy. Randy squinted, but that didn't help him make out any more details.

"Okay, here she is walking back to the flowers to see Violet," Frank said.

"Well, that's definitely Katie," Randy said. He couldn't believe she was here. His beautiful daughter had finally come home. Surely she had stopped by the market to buy flowers, gather ingredients to surprise them with a nice dinner, and pick up some peach tea and wine to bring back to the house. Randy let out a sigh. He just wanted to hold her. After all this time, he missed her so much. And now ... she was gone again.

"I wish the video quality was better so I could see her smile," Buck said. "I've missed that smile so mu—wait, did you guys see that?" He tilted his head and leaned closer.

Frank: "Where, Buck?"

"In the corner. It looked like the shadow of a person. Someone just out of sight."

"Let's replay that in slow motion," Randy said.

Frank rewound to the part where Katie was walking up to the flower stand and played it again frame by frame.

"There!" Buck said. "Did you see it?"

Frank replayed it several times, but they couldn't tell if it was a glitch or an actual silhouette of a person. "Tell you what," he said, "why don't we keep going with the rest of the video. If it's something important, it may show up again."

Randy's heart raced. On the screen, Frank brought Katie her coffee and muffin. As he walked away, he turned back around.

"That's where she told me not to tell you she was here because it was a surprise."

They watched as Violet walked away and Katie picked up the book of floral arrangements. The shadow appeared again, and a tall, thin man in a black shirt snuck up behind her and put his hand over her mouth.

All Randy wanted to do was reach through the screen and grab that creep before he could get to her.

"That's the same guy we saw on our front porch!" Randy said.

"Bastard!" Buck clenched his fists. "There it is. She's been kidnapped, Boss."

In the video, Tate shoved Katie toward the back of the store. A view from another camera showed them exiting through the employees-only door.

"Where does that door lead, Frank?" Randy asked.

Frank leaned forward. "Nowhere, really. It's just an emergency exit that goes out behind the store."

"Wouldn't opening it set off an alarm, though?" Buck asked.

"Normally, yes. But several years ago, our delivery drivers kept using it since it was the only back door we had, so we disabled the alarm."

"I'm getting the sense," Randy said, "that my daughter could be anywhere right now."

Matt paced back and forth on the deck. He needed to hear her voice, talk to her, tell her he was sorry for the way he'd acted and that for her, he would change and do whatever he needed to do to be with her.

But he knew what she would say. He remembered a conversation they'd had years ago when he was trying to get a job with one of the local farmers.

"He said my personality wasn't right for the job," Matt had told Katie. "I promised to make any changes he needed, but he still wouldn't hire me."

Matt would never forget what she said next as she took his face in her hands and looked right into his eyes. "You shouldn't change who you are for someone else for any reason, Matt," she'd said. "If they want you, they will want you the way you are. The way you are is what makes you special."

Matt picked up his phone and called her house, but he only got their voicemail.

"Katie, this is Matt. Again. Call me when you get this. I just want to know you're okay. Call me. Please."

"Any news, Peanut?" Maggie walked out onto the deck carrying a tray with sandwiches and glasses full of iced tea. She set it on the table and looked at Matt.

"No," he said. "I just called again and left a message." He picked up a glass of tea and took a sip.

"Well, I'm sure Randy or Katie will call when they get home. They haven't seen each other in quite a while, so they're probably out living it up right now."

He so badly wanted his mom to be right. But he ached not knowing.

◈

"Why are you doing this?" Katie asked Tate. "Why did you kidnap me and bring me here? Are you the one who's been stalking me and hanging around my house?"

She didn't understand. Every time she saw Tate at the store, she'd say hi and greet him with a smile. And he was always polite to her in return.

"Why would you do this to me?" Katie said, raising her voice. "I haven't ever done anything to you!"

"Yes, you have!" he screamed, standing over her. "You walk into my store and charm me with your kind words. You're so sweet, you dress so beautifully, and then you taunt me by coming in with another man on your arm." He leaned over and pointed his finger into her face. "So don't sit there and say you haven't ever done anything to me. You did. You broke my heart!"

Tate sat down and caught his breath. "But now," he said, lowering his voice, "you're no longer just a picture I can look at or a fantasy in my mind. You're mine now."

Katie wondered whether she would make it out of this alive. Clearly, Tate was obsessed with her. She knew that if she wanted to live, she'd have to talk to him in a calm and sweet manner. *Calm and sweet, Katie,* she told herself. *Calm and sweet.*

❧

Randy stormed out of the security office with Buck on his heels.

"Where are you going, Randy?" Buck said.

"I'm going to call in the forces and find my daughter, Buck!" Randy dug his phone out of his jeans pocket and dialed.

"Sergeant, this is Randy Calhoun. He has my daughter. That son of a bitch, that stalker, kidnapped her from Frank's store." He listened. "Yes, she *was* in California, but came home as a surprise. I'll fill you in on everything if you can meet us at the farm. Fifteen minutes? Okay, see you there."

"I'll stay here and review more of this footage," Frank said. "I'll call you if I find anything. Please keep me updated on this, guys. I want to help."

Back at the farm, Buck brought Katie's luggage into the living room while Randy dashed into the kitchen to see if Katie had called. The light on the answering machine was flashing. Randy pressed play.

"Hey Randy, this is Maggie Fuller. Sorry I missed you. I just wanted you to know that Katie left here in the middle of the night last night and didn't say a word. I just wanted to make sure she was okay. Give me a call back. Thanks. Bye-bye."

Randy's heart sank. "She must've called right after we left to go to the store."

He played the next message.

"Hey, it's Matt. Listen, if Katie is there, will you please tell her I'm sorry. I never meant to rush her or be selfish. It's just that ... I love her. Please call me back and let me know she's okay. Thank you."

There were three more messages from Matt. Randy turned around and looked at Buck, who was standing in the kitchen doorway.

"What are we going to tell them?" Buck said. "I mean, we have to call them back, right?"

Randy sighed. "Of course we do. And we will. But let's just wait until we get more information. They'll want to know what is being done, if

138

there's a search for her, that kind of thing," Randy said. "Let's just figure out a game plan first."

A loud knock at the front door broke the tension. Randy hurried to answer it. In his mind, it was Katie at the door, standing there with a big grin, holding flowers to greet him.

He opened the door with a smile, but it was Sergeant Haskins, not Katie. His smile faded and he invited him in.

"Have a seat, Sergeant," Randy said, motioning to the chair near the fireplace. Buck sat down on the couch, but Randy couldn't. The thought of Katie being out there dealing with God knows what right now was too unsettling for him.

Sergeant Haskins sat down and pulled out his notepad while Randy and Buck told him every detail they could think of about Katie's surprise visit, the abduction, and the security footage.

"Look," Randy said, wringing his hands, "I just want her home safe. Whatever it takes."

"I'll do everything in my power to bring your daughter home safe and sound, sir," Sergeant Haskins said. "It's my job. Me and my guys will head over to Frank's store now and check out the crime scene." He stood up and showed himself out.

"How about some coffee, Buck?" Randy asked, walking to the kitchen. "It's fixing to be a long evening."

Randy brewed a pot of coffee and poured two cups. He handed one to Buck then sat down at the kitchen table to call Maggie.

"Hello, Randy," she said. "How is Katie? We have been so worried about her."

How do I even start this conversation? he thought. He just blurted it out. "Katie is gone, Maggie." His voice cracked. "She was kidnapped. It happened at Frank's store, and we have footage of it. We can only assume it was the man who had been stalking her and showing up on our property."

His hands trembled, and tears welled up. Buck motioned for Randy to hand him the phone.

"Maggie, this is Buck. We've been in contact with the police, and they're going to be reviewing the tapes and trying to dig up anything they can find at the store. The main thing she needs right now is our support and prayers." Buck looked at Randy.

Randy could hear Maggie's voice quavering on the other end of the line.

"No," Buck said, "it's not your fault at all, Maggie. You didn't even

139

know she'd left."

⊷

"I guess you're right, Buck," Maggie said, "but I still feel at fault. Please keep us updated. Do you need us to come help with anything?" She looked at Matt, who had just sat down next to her. "Okay then, I'll wait to hear from you. Bye now."

She turned to Matt and told him what had happened.

"I'm going out there, Mom. Katie needs me. What an evil creep this guy is," Matt said, shaking his fist. "If you and Dad don't want to go, that's fine, but I need to be there."

CHAPTER TWENTY-TWO

The Fear Within

Katie grew cold as the fire died down and the sun's shadows gave way to dusk. Her thoughts turned dark.

No one is ever going to find me, she thought. *No one even knows I'm back in town, and the people that do were sworn to secrecy.*

Tate disappeared behind the wall and came back holding a tattered blanket. "Here, darlin'. You look like you could use this. The days are hot, but the cave is always cold."

She wrapped herself up as tightly as she could. "I still don't understand, Tate," she said, glaring at him. "Why are you doing this to me?"

Tate sighed. "All my life I was an outcast. I was picked on in school and I never had any friends. Hell, my parents didn't even want me around. I never had a girlfriend, either. But one day, you walked into the store and smiled at me. You actually spoke to me. After that, I went to work every day hoping I would see you there. I'd watch you meticulously pick out beautiful flowers. Flowers that paled against your beauty."

Tate leaned in and rubbed her cheek. His rough fingers on her skin sent a chill down her spine. "But then, you started coming in with *him*," he said. "You were no longer mine, and I was tired of being cast to the side because of my looks or my job or whatever reason people have for not giving me a chance. All I had then was the picture of you I'd taken from Frank's office. I would sneak over to your house to watch you, to be close to you. Even if it meant standing outside in a bush until your light went out."

He moved closer to her and sat down. His musky scent overwhelmed her. "No one ever gave me a chance in life or showed the least bit of courtesy except you. I mean, sure, Frank did, but he's my boss. He kind of has to."

She almost felt sorry for him. He had such a horrible life. "Is this where you live, Tate?"

He sighed and looked around at the room, then leaned forward and stoked the fire. "This place has been home to me for a while now," Tate said. "I have my parents' place, but who wants to go back to those memories? I get mail there, wash clothes, shower. But mostly, I'm here. This is the

141

place I feel safe."

Katie's heart broke for him. She couldn't imagine what it would be like never to feel at home even somewhere that was supposed to be home. Never to have the love you crave from your parents. To be alone all your life, thrown aside like a piece of trash. No human should feel that way or be treated that way. Did it give him the right to kidnap someone? No. But at least now she understood why he would do it.

Katie leaned forward and laid her hand on his back. He jumped, then turned to face her and took a deep breath.

"Tate, I'm sorry," she said in the softest tone she could muster. "I'm sorry you had to go through your life feeling like you didn't matter, like your whole existence was a sham."

She thought she saw tears in his eyes but wasn't sure. Tate jumped up and walked to the other side of the room.

"Anyway," he said, "are you getting hungry?"

Katie hadn't even thought about eating. She'd had half of the blueberry muffin at the store, but that was it.

"Maybe a little," she said, tightening the blanket around herself.

"I'll go find us some food," he said, putting on a jacket. "By the way, in case you're wondering, you won't be sleeping here tonight. I'll be taking you to my parents' house. You deserve a bed with a pillow to lay your head on." He zipped up his jacket.

Katie's mind leapt with excitement. *He's going to leave, and I'll be able to get out of here!* she thought, but then it dawned on her that it might not be the best idea. *If I leave now, he'll just continue to stalk me and terrorize me. If I run, I'll be in even more danger than if I stay. Then, we all may end up having to leave. I must stay to protect what we have. Plus, maybe his parents' place is closer to my house. At least then I'll be in familiar surroundings.*

As soon as Tate left the cave, she jumped to her feet. The sun had already set, and the fire didn't add much extra light to see by. She'd need a flashlight. She went around the wall to where Tate seemed to have everything stored. On top of a pile of firewood, she found a flashlight and switched it on. When she swung the beam around, her knees went weak.

Leaning against the cave wall was a shovel. Next to it lay a roll of duct tape and a coil of rope.

Her mouth went dry, and her heart pounded. "I'm not going to get out of this alive," Katie said aloud. "He's going to kill me."

142

❧

Randy sat on the front porch, looking up at the midnight sky and bright stars. Crickets chirped in the bushes nearby. He rocked back and forth in his chair, trying to comfort himself. Even though he was present physically, mentally he was elsewhere. Sleep would not be had that night, of that he was sure.

The front door opened, and Buck walked out.

"Hey, Boss," Buck said as he sat down. "You doing okay?"

Randy just looked at him. He felt miles away. His soul and spirit were broken. They'd been ripped away from him at the same time Katie was.

For several minutes, they sat in silence. "I'm going to say a prayer, Boss." Buck bowed his head. Randy reached out his hand and set it on Buck's knee. He couldn't hold back the tears.

"My girl," Randy said between broken breaths. "Pray for my girl." He buried his face in his hands.

Buck reached over and threw his arm around Randy's shoulder. He sat there with his arm around this shell of a man, while Randy sat wiping tears from his eyes. Then he cleared his throat and looked to the sky.

"You know, I haven't cried like that since I lost my wife," Randy said, forcing a smile. "This feels almost the same way. I can't talk to her face to face. I can't hug her or kiss her goodnight. I can only look at the stuff in her room and other things that remind me of her. Pictures on the wall hold her face, but I don't know if I will ever be able to again." His voice cracked.

"Don't talk like that, Boss," Buck said. "We will get her back. You've raised a strong young woman, and she's a fighter. She will do everything she can. I know it." He stood up and stretched. "Let's go inside and try to get some rest. If we aren't good to ourselves, we won't be any good for Katie. The police are searching high and low for her right now. If there's any news, we will be the first to know."

Randy took a deep breath and stood up. He was just about to follow Buck inside when a vehicle turned in and sped up the driveway. *Could this be Katie?* Randy thought. *The police? Who would be coming to see them?*

The bright headlights blocked any view of who it might be. The car skidded to a stop and the headlights turned off. The door opened, and

143

Frank Merriman stepped out.

"Frank?" Randy and Buck said in unison.

He ran up to them with a handful of papers. "Guys," he said, out of breath. "I need to show you this. I know who kidnapped Katie!"

✑

The roaring fire warmed Katie's face and cast a glow on the Chinese takeout boxes that littered the floor of the cave.

"How was dinner?" Tate said, wiping his lips with a napkin.

Katie patted her stomach. She was so full. It had been a long time since she'd eaten Chinese food and tasted the crunchy shell of an eggroll.

"It was delicious, Tate," she said, smiling. "Thank you so much for feeding me and making sure I am taken care of." *Calm and sweet.*

Inside, she trembled with fear. She couldn't stop thinking about what she'd seen on the other side of that wall. But she hoped that if she praised him and thanked him enough, he might see fit to keep her alive.

"Now that you have a full tummy, I bet you're ready to hit the hay for the night, huh?" Tate stood up and gathered their trash. She was tired. On top of all the events of the day, she hadn't slept very well the night before.

"What time is it, Tate?" Katie asked. She kicked herself for leaving her watch in her suitcase, but in her haste to pack this morning and leave without getting caught, she had taken everything on the nightstand and thrown it into her suitcase.

"It's eleven," Tate said.

Her dad was probably sound asleep right now, having sweet dreams and anticipating a phone call from her in the morning. *Wait a minute.* She froze. *Matt! By now, he's probably called my dad to tell him I was coming home. If that's the case, Dad and Buck probably went to Merriman's to pick up some dinner. And if Frank spilled the beans about me, they'll know something is wrong, and they'll come looking for me! I might be saved after all!* She smiled at the thought.

"You sure do have a pretty smile, Katie," Tate said. "What brought that on?"

Pull it together, Katie. Don't tip him off. She stood up and brushed

144

the crumbs from her jeans. "Just the thought of a good night's sleep in a comfy bed, of course."

⌁

Frank, Randy, and Buck sat at the kitchen table and spread all the papers out. They were printed photos that were taken from different cameras located throughout the store.

"I took the description of the man you guys saw," Frank said. "Then, I compared it to the man on the camera who took Katie. Now, we can't see his face, but the body and hair description match up to what you saw."

Randy and Buck looked at each other. "So, you're saying the guy that's been stalking my Katie is, in fact, the same man that has her now?"

"Precisely."

"Why in the hell are you so excited about *that*, Frank?" Buck said, his voice tinged with frustration.

"Because," Frank said, "I know who he is! He works for me, and you guys have actually met him. Remember that day I introduced you to the new hire, Randy?" Frank laid the last remaining photo on the table. "Fellas, meet Tate Stevens."

Randy pushed his seat back from the table and paced over to the sink. "That son of a bitch! Standing there talking to us like he didn't know us, while the whole time he'd been at our home watching our every move!" He slammed his hand down on the counter.

Frank walked over to him and put his hands on his shoulders. "I know you're upset, Randy, but at least now we know who he is, and we can track him down and put an end to this whole thing."

"No wonder he was so nervous all the time," Buck said. "I watched him one day while I was there. He just stood there twirling a loose thread from his—" Buck stopped. "That's it! The black thread from his shirt. Didn't they keep finding pieces of black string all over this place, Randy?"

Randy's eyes grew wide. "Yes, they did, Buck, and the string wrapped around the photo was black as well."

"It would only make sense, guys," Frank said. "He had access to my office and could easily have taken that photo off the board."

145

Randy pulled his phone out of his pocket. "I'm calling Sergeant Haskins. With this new information, maybe he can put together a search party."

Buck looked over at Frank, who was pouring himself some coffee. "You don't think he would hurt her, do you, Frank?"

Frank blew on his coffee and took a sip. "Well, I would like to think he wouldn't, Buck, but then again, I never tagged him as a psycho kidnapper either or I never would've hired him."

ॐ

Tate walked back behind the cave wall. Fear consumed Katie, because she knew what was behind that wall. She was too afraid to go on looking after she'd spotted the shovel, duct tape, and rope. Questions raced through her mind the longer he stayed back there, but she couldn't see a thing except for the flicker of his flashlight.

"Is he going to hit me with the shovel, tie me up, and tape my mouth? Or tie me up first and then hit me with the shovel?" Her thoughts ran wild assuming the worst.

Tate emerged, shovel in hand, and her whole body shook. She curled herself up into the tightest ball she could and prayed.

Marching around the room, he pushed all the candles and leaves off the ledges. Everything on the ground, he kicked to the side. Then he lifted the shovel high in the air. Just when Katie was sure he was about to hit her with it, he brought it down onto the fire pit, sending ashes and soot flying everywhere. Katie screamed and jumped up, her shrieks echoing through the cave. She backed up against the wall and faced Tate, who was still holding the shovel. He walked up to her and rubbed her face with the back of his hand. She shuddered.

"Don't worry, my love," he said in a low, breathy tone. "I would never, ever hurt you." He brushed the hair out of her face.

Katie didn't know what to think. This wasn't the Tate from ten minutes ago. He was even crazier, if that was possible. Almost as if a switch had flipped. He said he wouldn't hurt her, which should have eased her mind, but seeing him this way did not make her feel any better. In fact, it made her more terrified of what was going to happen.

146

He walked away from Katie and shoveled the ashes and remaining bits of firewood behind the wall. Then he tossed everything else into a large bag and lugged it out of the cave.

Maybe I should run now, she thought. *But if he caught up with me, what would he do?* She knew she didn't want to find out.

Tate hurried back in and glanced around, then grabbed Katie's arm and pulled her out of the cave.

He led her to his car, a beat-up, four-door sedan with a broken taillight that he had parked nearby. Dirty clothes filled the back seat, and the front floorboards overflowed with garbage.

She climbed into the front seat, careful not to sit on any of the soda-stained convenience store cups or plastic grocery bags full of trash. Trying her best to stay calm, she fastened her seatbelt and looked over at Tate.

"Where's your parents' house, Tate?"

"Don't worry, my love. It's not far at all." He handed her a ball cap and sunglasses. "Here, put these on. You're pretty popular in this town, and I don't want anybody recognizing you."

Katie complied, and off they went, leaving nothing but a cloud of dust behind.

At the kitchen table, Frank Merriman showed Sergeant Haskins the images his cameras had captured and recounted his version of what had happened that afternoon at the market.

"Can you give us access to your store so we can have a look around?" Sergeant Haskins said.

Frank reached into his pocket. "Have at it, sir," he said, tossing him a set of keys.

"This is a major lead, fellows," Sergeant Haskins said. He stood up and shook their hands. "I appreciate the phone call. I'll be in touch."

Randy walked him to the door while Buck stayed in the kitchen with Frank. Buck stretched and yawned.

"It's going to be a sleepless night, isn't it, Buck?"

Buck knew it was. Although he was exhausted, he was running on

147

adrenaline at this point.

Randy came back into the kitchen and clasped his hands together. "Gentlemen, here's how I see it. We haven't been doing anything except talking about what-if scenarios. That's not helping Katie in the least. I mean, what are we going to do, pace the floor all night until the phone rings or the sergeant comes back with news?"

Buck wanted Katie back safely in his arms as much as Randy did, and he knew they were both prepared to do whatever was necessary.

"I reckon you're right, Boss," Buck said, reaching for his keys on the counter. "Let's go find this guy and bring Katie home."

Frank's face lit up. "Let's do it, fellers!"

The three of them marched out of the house and piled into Randy's truck.

CHAPTER TWENTY-THREE

A House Divided

Matt's plane landed shortly after midnight. He had spent the entire flight wondering where Katie could be, and now he just felt drained and sick to his stomach.

In his back pocket was the note Katie had written to him. He blamed himself for this whole situation. If he hadn't acted so selfishly, she wouldn't be in danger right now.

From the airport, he hopped in a taxi and made it to the farm. Matt wasn't sure if anyone would be awake at this hour, but he didn't have anywhere else to go. He got out of the cab and walked up to the front porch. The house was dark except for the decorative candles glowing in the windows.

Wait a minute, he thought. *Did I see that right?* He turned around. Sure enough, there were no vehicles in the driveway.

"Man, I must be more tired than I thought," he said to himself, rubbing his eyes.

He walked the length of the front porch and around the side to see if Randy had parked in a different spot. Nothing. He picked up his phone and dialed the house number. A ring came from the kitchen phone, but no one answered. Surely if Randy were asleep, the ringing would have woken him up. He tried Randy's cell phone.

"Hello?" Randy answered in a breathless tone. He could hear noise and other voices in the background.

"Randy, can you hear me? It's Matt. I just got into town and I'm at your place. I want to help find Katie, but I have no idea where any of y'all are at."

"You have great timing, son, because that's what Frank, Buck, and I are out doing right now. I'll swing by and pick you up. The more eyes we have looking, the better. See you soon."

"Wait, Frank Merriman is with you?" Matt said. He was surprised. He'd never known Frank to be out past ten o'clock, much less up in the middle of the night.

"It's a long story, Matt, and we have all night to fill you in on

149

what's happened."

"Okay, I'll—" Matt started, but Randy had hung up.

Gone. That word echoed through his head. Katie was gone, and knowing that was difficult to stomach. But as he thought about how they were all pulling together to find her—even early-to-bed Frank—he grew more optimistic about their chances of bringing her back safely.

By the time Randy pulled up, he was more than just ready, he was pumped. He climbed into the truck, and they sped off.

∽

Katie hated that she couldn't see with the sunglasses on. She felt so lost and helpless and missed her dad and Buck more than ever. All she wanted was to feel the safeness and security that would come from being in her daddy's arms, smelling the sweet scent of his cologne, seeing his soft smile.

They were on the road for what seemed like forever before they finally stopped.

"Now look, Katie," Tate said as he pulled into a gas station. "I have to stop and fill up. I don't want you even thinking about making a move while we're here. Either you stay in the car, or I make you stay in the car. Understand?"

Katie only nodded in reply. She remembered what she'd found behind the wall in the cave, and a duct-tape bracelet was not something she wanted to be wearing. On the other hand, if ever there were a time to escape, it would be now.

Her heart raced as Tate pulled the car up to the gas pump. The overhead lights made it easier for her to see through her sunglasses, but she didn't recognize the gas station at all. That meant she wouldn't know anybody here, which made her even more nervous. No one to help her if she got out and ran.

But if she'd worked up the nerve to set off a fire alarm and empty a restaurant full of people, surely she could find the courage to run, right? She wondered if it would only make matters worse, though. Deciding to spare herself the heartache, she stayed in the car.

Tate opened the door and sat back down behind the wheel. "Good girl," he said as he leaned over and rubbed her face. "You listen well."

150

He laughed.

His personality changed the longer the drive went on and the far-ther outside of town they got, almost as if an even more sinister version of Tate was emerging.

"My place is right up the road here," Tate said, pointing ahead. "When we get there, I don't want any funny business, got it?"

She was petrified now. This wasn't the sweet, kind Tate she had been in the cave with. This was a new Tate, a mean Tate. His tone was harsh, his facial features as sour as month-old milk.

Katie nodded.

As she contemplated what to do, Tate turned into a dirt driveway and parked under some kind of roof. It was pitch dark outside, and she could barely see her hand in front of her face with the sunglasses on. Yet she didn't dare remove them.

Tate turned off the car and got out, then came around and opened her door. She stepped out.

"Put your hands behind your back," Tate said. "I don't want you getting any ideas of taking off."

Katie did as she was told. She cringed at the screech of duct tape as Tate pulled it off the roll and wrapped it around her wrists.

He opened the trunk and threw all the items he had brought from the cave onto the ground. The wind picked up, and she could hear what sounded like a tree limb scratching against a metal roof. *I feel like I've stepped straight into a horror movie*, she thought.

As they walked up to the house, a streetlight flickered on, helping her make out some of her surroundings. In the middle of the front yard sat a covered well, and next to it, a tall oak tree, overgrown and leaning to one side. The vines that covered the house had walked their way up the siding, over the eaves of the roof, and halfway up the crumbling brick chimney. She was scared to find out what the inside looked like with the outside in such distress.

As soon as they were inside, Tate reached for her face. She jumped.

"I just want to take your sunglasses off," Tate said, laughing. "Don't worry, my love. I won't hurt you. Unless I have to."

Katie didn't like the sound of that at all. She got the feeling she'd be stuck in this house for days.

"Tate," Katie said in the sweetest voice possible, "would you hap-pen to have a bathroom? I haven't been for quite some time. Will you undo my hands so I can go?"

"If I undo your hands," he said, "do you promise to go to the bathroom and come right back?"

Katie smiled. "Yes, Tate. I promise."

He cut the duct tape and led her to the bathroom. Just past the open foyer, they walked through the living room. It was surprisingly homey, with a plush, gray sofa and a coffee table that held magazines and newspapers. Paintings of snowy mountains and peaceful lakes adorned the walls. *But no pictures of family or friends,* she observed. *How sad.* In her opinion, that's what made a house a home.

He led her down a hallway with several doors that she thought must lead to bedrooms. All of the doors were closed except one.

"That's the bathroom," Tate said as he pushed the door open the rest of the way and turned on the light. "Come right out when you're finished."

She walked in and locked the door. Finally, a break from the insanity. A moment of quiet to clear her mind and devise a plan of escape. She looked around. Inside the bathroom, the walls were a light blue with several paintings of cabins and forests hanging on them. Above the bathtub was a dusty, dark-blue curtain covering a small window. *Jackpot!* Finally, the possibility of escape. But whether she'd fit through it was another story. Also, as old as the house was, she feared the window would make a racket if she tried to open it.

From outside the door, Tate called to her. "Hurry up, little lady. I have someone I want you to meet."

Someone to meet? There's someone else here?

Katie couldn't take one more minute of this. She looked again at the tiny window. Maybe she would fit, maybe she wouldn't, but she knew she had to try. She slid the curtain aside, only to discover the window had been boarded up.

She leaned against the wall and sank to the floor.

CHAPTER TWENTY-FOUR

Rhythmic Confusion

"Why don't we turn in for the night, guys?" Frank said, yawning. "At this point, we're so exhausted we probably wouldn't see Katie if she were right in front of our faces."

Buck was at the wheel now. They'd switched about an hour ago because Randy could barely hold his eyes open. From the back seat, Matt yawned and stretched.

Buck looked over at Randy. "What do you want to do, Boss?"

Randy took a deep breath. "Well, Frank is right. I haven't stayed up this late in years and my mind is nothing but a fog right now. I can't think of anywhere else she would be or could be anymore."

Buck made a U-turn and headed toward the house. "Maybe there will be some news from Sergeant Haskins come morning and we can get back to it," he said.

In the back seat, Frank's mind spun. He was thinking of how quickly everything had happened, almost as if it had been planned out in advance. *Katie gets back into town,* he thought, *and with no hesitation at all, Tate grabs her and they vanish without a trace? Truly bizarre.*

Back at the farm, the four of them sauntered into the living room.

"Make yourselves at home, guys," Randy said, yawning. "I know it's late and everyone is tired. Sleep wherever you'd like." He headed upstairs.

Buck walked to the kitchen to pour a glass of water while Matt and Frank sat on the sofa.

Matt turned to Frank. "Who was Tate, you know, when you hired him?" he said. "I mean, did he seem like a crazy man or what?"

Frank was a little offended that Matt thought he would hire a lunatic, but he also knew how blunt Matt could be at times. Plus, they were all running on no sleep and their nerves were frayed.

"I assure you, he didn't seem like a crazy man," Frank said. "He was quiet, sincere, had a good resume, and a clean record. He didn't send off any signals that concerned me or made me think he'd be a problem." He shrugged.

Buck walked back in with his glass of water and sat down in the re-

153

cliner. "We have to do something here, guys." He leaned forward. "Randy is beginning to lose it. I hate seeing him this way. You know, just this morning we were making plans to go out to California to surprise Katie." He took a sip of water. "It was a real blow to him when the reality of this kidnapping set in."

"We'll figure something out," Frank said. "I know a lot of people in this town, and it's an awfully small place to hide. Eventually, you will get run out of your rabbit hole."

"This is probably a dumb question," Matt said, "but has anyone tried calling her? It's a long shot, but maybe she has her phone with her, and we can call her and get her location that way."

"We didn't try that," Buck said, pulling his phone out of his pocket, "but when you're panicked, sometimes you forget the simple." He dialed.

Frank and Matt leaned toward Buck with looks of anticipation. A muffled buzzing sound came from the corner of the living room where Katie's suitcases were sitting. As the phone continued to ring, Buck walked over to her suitcase and unzipped the top pocket.

He took her phone out. "Call from Buck Brady," he said, reading the screen. "Dang. She must've put her phone in here when she got off the plane. I suppose you wouldn't need it if you're just grocery shopping."

"That's true," Frank said. "And I've never known Katie to be on her phone all that much."

As they lay back and rested their heads, none of them chimed in with any new ideas. After a few minutes, they were fast asleep.

The landline phone rang, piercing the silence. Buck struggled to open his eyes. Sunlight streamed through the living room window.

On the third ring, he made it out of the recliner and hurried to the kitchen to answer. A full pot of coffee sat on the counter next to an open carton of creamer. *Was that there last night?*

Focus, he told himself, picking up the phone. "Hello?"

"Is Randy there?"

He didn't recognize the voice. It was a male voice, but raspy and scratchy, almost like the caller needed to clear his throat. Buck looked over

154

at the pot of coffee again and wondered if he was dreaming.

"No," Buck said, "I don't believe he's here. May I ask who—"

Click. The line went silent.

Frank walked in. "Who was that?"

"I'm not sure," Buck said as he walked to the counter. "It wasn't a voice I knew, and it sounded strange. Before I could ask who it was, he hung up."

"Hey, guys," Matt said, walking into the kitchen. "Is Randy even here?" he asked, pointing at the pot of coffee.

Buck called his name and went upstairs to check. The door to his bedroom was open, his bed empty but unmade.

"His truck is still out front!" Matt yelled from downstairs.

They went outside and checked around the side of the house and in the backyard, then walked down to the barn. There, they found Randy sitting on a bale of hay, coffee in hand.

"What's up, Boss?" Buck said. "Are you okay?"

Randy leaned forward. "I've just been thinking is all. I haven't heard a word from Sergeant Haskins since last night. I know that's not a long time, but it feels like a lifetime to a parent. Knowing she could be in danger, not hearing anything is killing me."

❧

Frank spoke up. "Randy, we just received a call from—"

Matt held up his hand. "Guys, do you hear that? I think I hear the phone ringing inside."

They all sprinted back to the house. Randy was the first one into the kitchen, and he scooped up the handset.

"Hello? Randy speaking," he said, trying to catch his breath.

"I know where your daughter is, Randy," the voice said.

Randy stood holding the phone with his mouth open wide while Frank, Buck, and Matt stared at him. Randy switched on the speakerphone so they could all hear.

"Your daughter is there, just beyond the trees," Tate said. "Get to her fast or he will make her bleed. Pass the old station where your car will get gas. Get to her, Randy, and get to her fast!" He yelled the word "fast."

155

Click. "Oh my gosh," Randy said as the reality of the situation sank in. "Katie's in real danger, and I have absolutely no idea where she is."

"Call Sergeant Haskins and tell him what happened," Buck said. "Then let's go find Katie."

❧

Matt was almost out the door when Frank told him to wait. "We don't even know where we're going yet," Frank said as Matt came back into the kitchen. "Why don't we sit down and figure this out first."

Randy hung up with Sergeant Haskins, then unfolded a map and spread it out across the kitchen table as they all gathered around.

"Okay, here's where we are," Randy said, pointing to the map.

"That means my store would be about here," Frank said. "Behind the store, you have some land." Frank circled the area with his finger.

"So that's where we should go then, right?" Matt asked. "I mean, what was it this Tate guy said? 'Your daughter is just beyond the trees.' If there's land behind the store, there's bound to be some trees, right?"

"Well, I think that's a good start," Buck said, "but there's no gas station nearby, is there, Frank?" He leaned over the map to look more closely.

"You're right," Frank said. "Tate—assuming that's who this is—said to pass the old station where you get gas. But there isn't a gas station for another twenty, twenty-five miles going in that direction."

Randy walked over to the counter and poured himself more coffee. "Sergeant Haskins is on his way over now," he said, taking a sip. "I think until he gets here, we need to stay put."

Buck jumped up. "Katie is in trouble, Randy! You heard what that madman said. Get to her fast or he'll make her bleed!"

Randy put his hand on Buck's shoulder and looked him in the eyes.

"I know you're scared, Buck. We all are. But if we go on some wild goose chase and happen to find this guy, we might spook him and make the situation even more dangerous. Then Katie would be in even bigger trouble. Let's let the police do their jobs. They're trained to handle people like this. If we go barging in, we could get her hurt. Or God forbid, worse."

156

❧

"Please, have a seat," Randy said, showing Sergeant Haskins into the living room.

In his hand were several Manila folders, which he set on the coffee table as he took a seat on the sofa.

"Here's what we know, guys," he said, opening the first folder. "We went to your store, Frank, and ran over all the footage. Our evidence techs took fingerprints, which were all over the back door, and they're being analyzed right now." He picked up one of the documents to show them. "We also canvassed the area behind the store, and on a tree back there, we found strands of auburn hair, which we think might be Katie's."

"So what about the phone call?" Randy said. "What do you make of that?"

"Well," Sergeant Haskins said, "first, I'd like to rule out that it was just someone playing a prank. Does anyone else know that she's been kidnapped?"

They all looked at each other and shook their heads. "Not that I know of," Matt said. "Besides my parents, of course."

"Randy, if it's okay with you," Sergeant Haskins said, "I would like to tap your phone line. That way, if whoever that was calls back, we can pinpoint where the call is coming from."

"That would be fine, Sergeant. Whatever you need to do."

Sergeant Haskins stood up and collected his folders. "I'll have my guys on this as soon as possible. Call me if you hear anything else." He shook all their hands and left.

In the living room, Buck paced, almost in circles. He couldn't stand not doing anything at all while Katie could be getting hurt as they spoke. He looked at the picture of Katie's mom on the wall. A real person, beloved by her family and friends, who was now only a framed memory. He didn't want the same fate for Katie.

"Listen, guys," he said. "If there were strands of her hair found be-

157

hind the store, that means she was back there for sure. We need to go see if we can find something, anything, they may have missed." He looked over at Randy for his reaction.

Randy took a deep breath and let it out. He looked around the room then down at the floor. After a few seconds he looked back up. "Well? What are y'all waiting for?" He stood up. "Let's go."

CHAPTER TWENTY-FIVE

The Chase

Katie awoke with a start, not realizing she'd fallen asleep.

Where am I? she thought. *How long have I been out?*

The dingy bathroom came into focus. She must have dozed off against the wall.

She rose to her feet. Where was Tate? And why wasn't he trying to get in? She stood at the sink and washed her hands, then splashed cold water on her face. The last thing Tate had said to her was that he wanted her to meet someone. Was it another girl he had kidnapped? A family member he didn't tell her about? Or someone else altogether, like an accomplice? Maybe he wasn't the only one who had been lurking around their farm.

Katie opened the bathroom door and peeked out. Silent. She padded down the hallway, dragging her finger along the wall as she walked. The dark hallway and quiet house put her on edge.

She opened a door off to the left and felt around for the light switch. A single, bare light bulb on the ceiling came on and cast a glare on the lifeless concrete walls. Against the far wall sat a tattered sofa riddled with patches, none of which matched the color of the sofa. A fireplace on one side of the room featured a dark wooden frame that would have looked nice were it not marred by deep scratches, as though some ferocious creature had dug its claws into it. A worn area rug lay on the scuffed hardwood floor in front of the hearth.

The lone window was boarded up. The fact that this room hadn't seen the sun in ages made her feel sad and even more hopeless than she felt already. She turned off the light and backed out of the room.

Still, where was Tate? At the end of the hallway was a large area that could have been a second living room. Flipping on the light revealed a stained, black futon shoved against the far wall with a TV tray in front of it, and across from it, a rickety wooden table that held a small, dusty television. In the corner sat another table with two stools in front of it. On top were a single electric burner and a pan.

This must be where he cooks and eats, Katie thought. *No wonder he likes hanging out in that cave. This place is a dump.*

159

Just then, a loud growling sound came from behind one of the doors farther down the hallway. Terrified, she walked toward the sound, almost as if her body were forcing her to take each step against her will. A scraping sound on the door only heightened her fear. Something was trying to claw its way out.

"Get down!" Tate yelled from inside the room. "Get away from the door!"

His footsteps grew closer and heavier. With each footfall, she trembled even more.

Tate cracked the door, but it was forced open by a hulking Doberman Pinscher that tore out of the room and bolted toward Katie. She ran down the hall screaming and jumped onto the futon.

"Down, boy!" Tate grabbed the leash and yanked the massive dog back as it snarled at Katie.

⁊

Randy, Matt, and Frank scoured the area behind the store where the police had found strands of Katie's hair. Buck, meanwhile, had wandered off into the trees.

"Guys, come up here!" came Buck's faint voice from the top of the hill.

They walked up and saw him standing next to the entrance of a cave. "I'm going to take a peek inside," Buck said.

He stepped into the entrance passage. Frank followed, and together they ventured into the main room.

"Doesn't look like there's anything here," Frank said, sweeping his phone's flashlight around the room.

Buck walked behind the wall on the other side of the room. "Someone's been here, Frank!" He came back holding a takeout box from a Chinese restaurant. "And from the looks of this place, they left in a hurry."

Back outside the cave, Buck showed the container to Matt and Randy.

"How do we know it's hers, though?" Matt said. "It could have been here for a long time. Or maybe brought in by bears or something."

"Let me see that," Randy said, walking over to Buck and inspecting the container.

"I'm with Buck on this one, Matt. There's no way this box has been here long. And if a bear had brought it in, it would be all torn up. No, this is recent."

Matt shrugged. "Maybe you're right. Anyway, I'm going to take a look around the other side of the cave." He walked off.

"Frank, didn't you say there was a gas station about half an hour from here?" Randy said.

"Yeah. Do you want to head over—"

"You guys, come check this out!" Matt shouted from back in the trees. They looked at each other, then scrambled toward Matt's voice.

Matt beckoned them over with one hand and pointed at the ground with the other. "Look at this! Tire tracks!"

Randy crouched down to get a closer look. "I'll be damned," he said. "That psycho must have brought Katie into the cave, had Chinese food for dinner, then taken her somewhere else."

"But where?" Frank said.

"Yes," Randy said, "that's the million-dollar question."

"Tate said something about a gas station," Frank said. "What were the words he used?"

Buck, in fact, remembered word for word what Tate had said. He'd been replaying those words over and over in his mind, especially the part about making her bleed. Words he'd never forget, spoken in a voice he didn't want to remember.

"Pass the old station where your car will get gas." Buck stared at the ground and ran his fingers through his dark, wavy hair.

"Let's try to find that gas station, boys," Randy said.

"Hand me that food box, Randy, and I'll put it in a grocery bag just in case it has fingerprints on it," Frank said.

They walked back down the hill to the truck and piled in.

"I'll call Sergeant Haskins now and let him know what we found," Randy said from the driver's seat. He dialed the number and switched to speakerphone.

161

Two rings. "Haskins."

"Sergeant, it's Randy Calhoun." He told him about the cave, the Chinese food box, and the tire tracks.

"Randy, listen carefully. Do not, I repeat, do not go searching for her yourselves," Sergeant Haskins said. They all froze, looking around at each other inside the truck. "We have no idea what this guy is capable of, and we need to stay levelheaded. I don't want you guys, Katie, or any of my men and women hurt. Do you understand me?"

"Of course, Sergeant. We're all just on edge. Thank you again. See you soon." Randy hung up.

They fell silent after hearing Sergeant Haskins's stern warning.

"Well, I say we go anyway," Matt said. "Who knows when they'll get to her, and by then it may be too late."

Randy turned around and looked at him. "I get it, Matt," he said. "I do. And I feel the same way. I want to go in, guns blazing, and yank her out of there. But we can't, okay? We just can't. Sergeant Haskins is right. We will be putting her life and ours on the line if we do that." He turned back around and stared out the windshield.

Buck chimed in. "Matt, we haven't always seen eye to eye on things, and I do know how you feel, but—"

"How could you possibly know how I feel, Buck? She didn't live with you for over a month. You didn't kiss her lips every night before bed and see her for breakfast every morning. You didn't hear her laugh or feel her soft touch the way I did all those years back. You weren't going to propose to her either, so don't you sit there and tell me you know how I feel, because you *don't*!"

Matt turned away and looked out the window.

"Propose?" Randy said, turning back around. "You proposed to her, Matt?"

"No, I didn't. I was going to, but ..." Matt stopped. "Well, it's a long story, and it doesn't matter now. It's not me she's in love with anymore. It's Casanova up there that she wants."

Buck's heart raced and he tried to hide a smile. *She loves me?* That made him more impatient than ever to see her again and find out if it was true.

A few minutes later, Sergeant Haskins pulled up in his SUV and got out.

"I want this whole area searched," he told his officers as they filed out of their patrol cars, then walked over to Randy's truck. Frank stepped

162

out and handed him the bag with the Chinese food box.

"This was found in the cave, sir," Frank said. "We're guessing he took her in there, had dinner, then dragged her off somewhere else."

Sergeant Haskins looked into the bag. "We'll send this off as well. Good work, guys. Now," he said, opening his notepad, "let's talk about this Tate Stevens and what he said."

"He said she was beyond the trees and then past the station where your car will get some gas," Randy told him. "Frank said there's a gas station about half an hour from here, which we believe is the one he's talking about."

"That's Old Man Dooley's gas station," Matt said. "When I was here last month, I stopped by and saw him. He said he's there practically all the time now after his wife passed. He's bound to have seen them."

Sergeant Haskins flipped his notepad closed. "Okay. Let's go talk to Old Man Dooley and ask him if he saw anything."

He told some of his officers to stay and keep searching, and the others to get back in their cars and follow Randy to the gas station.

A man with neatly trimmed, gray hair walked outside and watched as the convoy pulled into the gas station. He lifted his glasses, which were almost too big for his face, squinted, then set them back down. Today, like most days, he wore bib overalls and an old trucker's hat.

"What in the Sam heck is going on here?" Old Man Dooley asked as Matt walked up to him and shook his hand.

"Do you remember the friend I was telling you about a while back?"

"Well, sure I do. Real pretty girl, I remember you saying."

"Yes, sir." Matt pointed to all the cars. "We're here because we thought you might be able to help us. My friend has been kidnapped, and we believe she and her kidnapper came through here last night."

He stared at Matt and raised one eyebrow. "Kidnapped?"

Sergeant Haskins walked up, introduced himself, and shook Old Man Dooley's hand. "Sir, do you remember anyone coming through here late last night?"

Old Man Dooley took off his hat and rubbed his brow. "I was here for sure," he said. "I don't go home much anymore. It just hurts too bad."

He paused for a few moments, then continued. "I do remember a car in the middle of the night. They didn't come inside, but I recall lookin' out the window just as they was turnin' into the lot. You know, young folk don't get enough sleep these days. It baffles me."

"You say you looked out the window," Sergeant Haskins said, pulling out his notepad. "Did you see the driver or passenger? Any idea what kind of car it was?"

"Oh yeah, I did. I don't know the exact car. They all look the same to me nowadays, but it was a dark color. The driver was a young fella, real thin, dark hair."

"Great," Sergeant Haskins said, scribbling it down. "Did you see a passenger by chance?"

"I seen another person in the car, but I can't tell you if it were a guy or girl. They had on a ball cap and sunglasses. It made me wonder if they'd been drinkin', wearin' them sunglasses in the middle of the night and all."

Sergeant Haskins motioned toward the road in front of the station. "Did you happen to see which way they turned?"

"They sat there for a while waitin' to pull out, and then took a right out of here." He pointed down the road. "But after that I couldn't tell you."

Sergeant Haskins shook Old Man Dooley's hand. "You've given us a wealth of information, sir, and I thank you for your cooperation."

"Yes, thank you," Matt said, also shaking his hand.

"So, what's the game plan, Sergeant?" Randy asked when he walked up to the truck.

"We have a pretty good idea that it's the same man. He said the passenger was wearing a ball cap and sunglasses, but he couldn't tell who it was. Appears they just got gas and left."

Matt climbed into the truck. "They took a right out of here," he said. "There aren't too many places back that way. Just a few small neighborhoods."

"Tell you what, Matt," Sergeant Haskins said, "You guys lead the way, and we'll follow. I admit it's a bit backwards, but this is out of my district, and you know it better than me. But if you see any car that resembles the one he described, you put your hazards on and let us take over. Deal?"

"Deal," the four of them said in unison.

CHAPTER TWENTY-SIX

Delusional Dilemmas

The dog continued to bark and growl at Katie. Fearing Tate would lose his grip on the leash and the dog would lunge at her, Katie jumped off the futon and hid under the table in the corner of the room, using the two stools to shield her.

"I'm sorry, Katie. We never have company, so he doesn't know any manners." With a jerk of the collar and a stern warning to be quiet, Tate managed to calm the animal down. "I won't let him hurt you. Please come out."

Katie crawled out from under the table and stood up. She walked across the room, keeping her eye on Tate and the dog, then sat back down on the futon.

"His name is Mars," Tate said. "I've had him since I was a boy. I named him Mars because, as corny as it may sound, I thought he was out of this world. He was the only one who cared about me back then. Honestly, he probably still is."

Tate let go of the leash, and Mars walked over to Katie and sniffed around.

"Is this who you wanted me to meet, Tate?" Katie asked, running her hand over the top of Mars's head. She loved his soulful, brown eyes and soft fur. He licked her hand.

"Yes. But you were in the bathroom for so long, I gave up."

"You seem to take really good care of him."

"Of course," he said. "Mars and I, we take care of each other. I'm all he has, and he's all I have." He looked at Katie and smiled. "That is, until now. Now, we have you."

"What do you mean by that?" Katie asked. A chill ran down her spine.

"I mean you're mine now. I finally have you here, and they can't take you away. You, me, and Mars, we can be a family now. The family I never had."

So that's what it is, Katie thought. *He wants a family. He chose me because I was nice to him and showed him compassion.*

165

"That's not how it works, Tate. You can't keep me here against my will and force me to be your family."

"*Yes, I can!*" he shouted. Katie froze, eyes wide. He lowered his voice. "I saw how great your family was and I wanted the same thing for myself. I know how you hold everything together at your house. I saw how you guys got along and played games and had cookouts. You loved each other, laughed with each other. Then I saw how lost your dad and that Buck guy were with you gone. They got to feel what I feel all the time."

"Why did you keep coming around even after I'd left town? What the hell, Tate?" She couldn't hide her anger anymore. "How long were you spying on our cookouts and peeking through our windows, anyway?"

"Calm down, darling. I'm not trying to make you angry. I was just waiting for you to come back. But the stinking cops kept coming over, poking around in my hiding spots, trying to find stuff I'd left behind. But guess what? I got the last laugh, because they never found me."

"They will, Tate," she said. "My father is a very persistent man, and he'll stop at nothing. I promise you he will find me."

"Nope, not gonna happen," he said, shaking his head. "I won't allow it."

Mars lay down at Tate's feet and looked up at him. Tate set a treat on the floor, and it was gone in two bites.

Tate looked at Katie. "Are you hungry, darling? I'll fix you breakfast."

What just happened? Katie thought as she stared at Tate. *He went from screaming at me to offering me food?*

"Tate, we have to be real," Katie said. "You can't force this fake family. It's never going to happen."

Tate stopped in his tracks and glared at Katie. Mars let out a quiet growl.

"Come on, Mars, I don't want you to have to see this." He took Mars down the hall and put him back in his room. He walked back to Katie and got so close to her that she could feel his warm, stale breath on her face.

"That's not for *you* to decide," he hissed. "Do you hear me? You're mine now, and there's nothing you or your dear old pops can do. We are a family now. Not you and your dad, not you and Buck, not you and *anybody*!"

He was shouting now. What frightened her most was how quickly his demeanor had changed. Looking into his eyes was like staring straight into his murky soul. The smell of his cologne nauseated her.

"It's me, you, and Mars, and we are going to live happily ever after!"

166

It took all of Katie's strength to hold back the tears. Her nose burned and her eyes watered as intense anger welled up in the pit of her stomach. She clenched both her fists.

"No way that's going to happen," she said.

"I suggest you stop talking before I do something I will wholeheartedly regret," Tate said. "I don't want to hurt you, but if it makes you listen, I will."

"Oh yeah, Tate?" Katie couldn't take it anymore. "And if I don't?"

Tate gave her a cold, empty stare. She almost felt as if he could suck the soul right out of her body.

"Mess around and find out, my dear," he yelled. "Now be quiet!"

Katie wanted to punch him right in the face. But she knew that with the way his moods were changing from one minute to the next, she would only be tempting fate. The last thing she needed was to get hurt with no idea of when—or even if—someone would be there to help her.

❧

With Sergeant Haskins and his officers in tow, Randy made yet another turn onto yet another street. They'd already wound their way through several neighborhoods, and he was losing hope.

"She's here somewhere, Randy," Buck said. "We've still got a few more streets to check."

Randy reached over and patted Buck's shoulder. "You're right. Let's just keep our eyes peeled and we'll—"

"There it is!" Frank yelled from the back seat. "I see the car! Right there in that old metal barn."

"Oh wow," Matt said from the back seat. "That's Derek Stevens's old place."

Buck: "You know them?"

"I bet everybody does, even Randy."

"I know them?" Randy said.

"Yeah, sure. A while back he caused a big stink when he started a fight with one of the local farmers in town. Threatened to burn his farm down. Remember that? I heard he was an abusive man back then, too. Real angry type. I guarantee you Tate is his son, and no doubt inherited his

167

father's temper."

Randy flipped his hazard lights on as they approached the house. Within seconds, he got a call from Sergeant Haskins.

"Is it the house with the big tree and the well in front?"

"Yes, it is. Please be careful, though, because I just found out the family that lives there has a history of violence."

"We won't let anything happen to Katie," Sergeant Haskins said. "I promise. Keep driving to the end of this street and around the corner. We'll meet up there and formulate a plan."

⁊

Tate plugged in the electric burner and set the pan on top. He took some eggs and sausage out of the refrigerator and slammed it shut.

The aroma from the sizzling sausage was making Katie hungry. The Chinese food was now a distant memory, and she knew she'd need to eat to make it through the day. The problem was that she didn't trust Tate. It would be so easy for him to slip something into the eggs and knock her out.

Is this how it was when he was a kid? she wondered. *Did he fear his parents the way she feared him now?* She wanted so badly to move on from this nightmare and go home. But one horrifying thought wouldn't let her out of its grip: *What if Tate is right, and they never find me?*

⁊

"Our best bet is to throw a flash bomb," Sergeant Haskins declared. They had all huddled around him as he explained the plan of action. "That will catch him by surprise, and we'll use the opportunity to gain entry and get Katie out before he has a chance to do anything. What we don't know is whether he has any weapons."

Buck spoke up. "And given how brazenly he kidnapped her in a public place in the middle of the day, you can bet he won't easily give her up."

"I agree with Buck," Frank said. "He did good work at the store for me, but he was a fidgety, nervous mess before this happened. Who knows how long he'd been after her before he slipped up and made her aware of his presence. He's clearly delusional, and that makes him all the more dangerous."

Randy walked up to Sergeant Haskins. "Whatever you decide to do, sir, I trust your judgement to make sure my little girl is safe. I need her."

CHAPTER TWENTY-SEVEN

Love Conquers All

Buck walked away from the huddle and leaned over a fence that separated the neighborhood from a large field just beyond.

"Hey, Buck." Matt walked up behind him.

"Hey, Matt."

"Listen, I know we haven't been getting along very well, but I just wanted to say ... I think the two of you will make a fine couple. And I also know that Katie ... well, she's going to be okay," Matt said. He motioned toward the officers. "These guys have some really good ideas on how to get her out, and this ain't their first time doing it."

Buck sighed and looked at Matt. "Did she really say she loves me?"

Matt leaned against the fence next to Buck. "She didn't say the words, but I saw it in her eyes when we were talking about how homesick she was. That's when she ran out in the middle of the night to come home. She was so determined to get back to you and Randy that she called a cab, put herself on a plane, which she isn't fond of, by the way, and flew for hours by herself to be with y'all again. So yeah, even though the words 'I love Buck' didn't come out of her mouth, her actions screamed it." He chuckled.

That brought a smile to Buck's face, and he couldn't wait to finally be able to hold Katie and tell her that he loved her too.

His heart was aching inside. He remembered when he first met Katie. She was fresh out of high school and raring to take on the world. She'd always said that she would never date one of her dad's helpers, and she'd turned him down every time he asked for a date. So instead, he would watch her feed the animals or break horses while he loaded hay. He would enjoy the quiet times with her, drinking tea in the evenings and coffee in the mornings. For him, those were special times, and now, those memories were keeping him going.

"Thanks, Matt. That's really decent of you," Buck said as he shook his hand. "And thanks for stepping up to take care of her this past month."

Behind them, Sergeant Haskins was wrapping things up. "Okay, everyone, let's get our gear together and go take care of business." He

171

looked at Frank and Randy. "You guys hang back. We don't want to put you in any danger."

"Understood," Randy said. "But can we pray before you go in there? I mean, if anybody can get everyone home safe, it's God."

They formed a circle, joined hands, and prayed for the safety of Katie and the officers. After the prayer, Frank, Buck, Randy, and Matt watched the police cars speed off down the street.

"What do you say we go wait in a place where we can see what's going on?" Randy said.

"You sure that's a good idea?" Frank said.

"I think if we stay far enough away, it'll be fine," Buck said. "Plus, I would like to be there when they bring her out of the house."

They climbed in the truck and Randy parked a few houses down. There, they could see most of what was going on, but remained out of sight. As the police moved to surround the house, they rolled the windows down so they could hear everything.

⚘

"Breakfast is served, darling," Tate said as he handed her a plate piled high with sausage and scrambled eggs. "Please, do come eat with me. I know you're hungry."

Katie's stomach was in knots, her brain in a fog. She couldn't think complete thoughts anymore and was angry at herself for ditching Matt in the middle of the night and putting herself in this predicament.

Why, oh why, she thought, *couldn't I have just stuck it out a little longer in California? I would be safe, and Lord knows I could use another one of those spa days.*

Tate's flipping and flopping moods were not helping, either. One minute he was in her face threatening her, and the next minute he was offering her breakfast. A combination of stress, anger, fear, and no sleep were causing so much frustration in her that all she could do was stare off into space, not uttering a word in reply to Tate's offer of breakfast. She was retreating into her own little world, a world that was safe and where love surrounded her. Knowing the world outside these cold walls was still alive and happy brought her solace, but as each minute passed, a good outcome seemed more and more in doubt.

"I said, breakfast is served!" Tate yelled.

Clank! He slammed his fork down on his plate and skittered over to the futon, where she sat staring straight ahead at the empty wall. He seized her arm and yanked her up off the bed. Pain seared through her shoulder, and she screamed as he dragged her across the room and threw her onto one of the stools in the corner.

"I said eat with me, and that's what I meant!" Tate's face was bright red.

From inside his room, Mars growled and scratched at the door.

Trembling, Katie picked up her fork and tried her best to scoop some eggs with it. As she lifted the fork to her mouth, the smell of rotten eggs hit her. She looked at Tate, who was staring at her as if he expected her to eat them. The second she placed the eggs in her mouth, she gagged.

"Does my cooking repulse you, Katie?" he whispered, then raised his voice. "Well, does it?"

She shook her head.

"Swallow them, Katie. Swallow them now!" His voice was now a high-pitched wail.

For Katie, rotten eggs were the last straw. This guy had made her feel unsafe in her own home. He'd made her put her life on hold for months. He'd taken her away from her family and had now caused her physical pain. Her arm, no doubt bruised, was throbbing. And now he wanted her to swallow rotten eggs? *Uh-uh.*

She smiled as sweetly as she could, inhaled, then spit the eggs into his face.

"No, Tate," she said. "You eat them."

He jumped off his stool and grabbed a paper towel. As he wiped the eggs off his face, he paused and looked at her.

His arm flew out at her, and with the back of his hand he slapped her across the face. She fell to the floor. Blood trickled from her lips.

Tate stood over her. "I told you I wouldn't hurt you if I didn't have to. But you made me have to. Me hitting you is your fault, Katie." He leaned over to grab her.

A surge of adrenaline shot through her, and she jumped up off the floor to face him. He grabbed both of her arms, one in each hand, but she fought him with all the force she could muster.

He seemed taken aback by her strength, but he overpowered her, twisting both of her arms behind her back. He pulled her backwards down the hallway, into one of the rooms, and over to a dresser. He flung open one of the drawers and pulled out a gun. She could feel his heart pounding against her back as he pointed the gun at her head.

"You're going to regret all of that, Katie," Tate seethed. "How dare you be like them. You're supposed to be different. You're supposed to love me!"

Frenzied barking came from Mars's room as Katie tried to wrestle herself away, but she was no match for Tate.

"Help me, somebody!" she sobbed. "Please help me! He's going to kill me!"

Katie was certain her screams were in vain. She had no idea the cavalry was right outside, hearing her every cry for help.

***

The police surrounded the house. Sergeant Haskins and three of his men were at the front door, with the other officers stationed at the windows.

From where they were parked up the street, Randy could hear loud barking.

"Dog!" one of the officers yelled. "We got a dog in there!"

Sergeant Haskins drew his gun. The guys all got out of the truck to watch the action unfold.

"This is it," Buck said. "That dog must have pushed them into action."

Randy was a nervous wreck. This didn't seem to be going as planned.

"What's going on?" Randy asked, placing his hands on his head.

Matt walked up beside him and put his hand on his shoulder. "It'll be okay, Randy. She'll be fine. She's a strong woman. Just keep remembering that."

***

"What the hell is Mars so worked up about?" Tate muttered as he pulled the curtain aside and peeked through a small crack in the board. Police officers were all over his property. He gasped.

"They've come for me, haven't they, Tate?" Katie said. "They're here! Thank you, God, they're here!"

"One move from them, Katie, and you're toast. You got it?" Tate's voice quavered.

Even though Katie was more terrified than ever, she forced herself to remain calm and think clearly.

"Tate, you don't want to do this," Katie said. "You love me, right? If you kill me, you'll never have me again."

"You're right. I do love you, and I never wanted to hurt you, darling." He glanced back at the window. "But if I can't have you, then neither can they!"

"Tate," came a deep voice over a bullhorn. "This is Sergeant Haskins with the Orange Grove Police Department. Your house is surrounded. We know you are in there and we know Katie is, too. Surrender now and no one gets hurt."

Tate tugged at the top corner of the rotting window board and snapped it off, then smashed several of the windowpanes with the butt of his gun.

"You're right," he shouted back. "I have Katie, and I also have a gun to her head. If you guys come in here, she's a goner. Understand me? She's finally mine, and I won't let you guys have her." He tipped his head back and roared with laughter.

The guys could hear Tate's voice, even from a few houses away. Randy leaned against the truck and buried his head in his hands. "He's going to kill her. He's going to kill her."

Fire tore through Buck's veins when he heard that. No way was he going to stand by and let the woman he loved get murdered by this lunatic. He charged down the street and right into Tate's front yard.

"You want to kill somebody, Tate? Here I am!" Buck screamed at the top of his lungs.

Sergeant Haskins and the other officers ran off the porch, yelling

175

for him to leave and take cover. Buck didn't listen.

Just then, the front door opened. Tate had a gun pointed at Katie's head. Katie's face was covered in black and blue marks, her lips coated with dried blood, and her eyes wide with terror. Tate pulled the gun away and aimed it straight at Buck.

"See? It's that simple," Buck said, not flinching. "I don't want her hurt, and I know you don't, either. Let her go, Tate. Katie doesn't deserve this, and you know it. She's the only one who ever showed compassion for you, and look at what you've done. Her face is marked by your hands. You've only made her afraid of you."

As Buck spoke, the officers inched closer to the front porch. Tate didn't seem to notice. He pointed the gun back at Katie.

"You don't want to kill her," Buck said. "You love her. And so do I."

Katie sobbed. "Tate, please. Let me go."

"I'm sorry, my love. I can't do that, especially now." He pointed the gun at Buck again. "Okay, one of two things is going to happen. Either you leave my property right now or you leave in an ambulance because I *will* shoot you."

"You know I won't just walk away, Tate. The only way I'm going to leave is with Katie in my arms. Now let's be civil about this. Just put the gun down and this whole ordeal can be over."

Katie was terrified for Buck. Without moving her head, she looked around for something she could grab and smash over Tate's head. That's when, out of the corner of her eye, she spotted him standing there, just up the street.

Daddy! Her heart jumped.

Randy's whole body shook with fear, not only for Katie, but for Buck as well.

Would I be willing to stand in front of a gun for Katie the way Buck is right now? he thought to himself.

Then he heard it. Loud and clear, from the front door.

"Daddy, I love you!"

❧

That was just the distraction the police needed. Her shout caught Tate off guard, and he loosened his grip on her. An officer sprinted up to the front door and tackled him.

As Tate staggered backward, the gun went off. Buck sank to the ground and lay there motionless. While several officers ran to subdue Tate, Sergeant Haskins ran over to Buck.

Katie ran over, too, and knelt over him. "Buck, baby, don't leave me. Please. I love you. I need you." Tears spilled from her eyes as she ran her fingers through his dark hair.

Randy, Matt, and Frank all ran over. Katie stood up and threw her arms around her dad. She buried her head in his chest and sobbed as he held her.

"He's breathing!" Frank said.

Katie let go of her dad and dropped to her knees beside Buck. "Please talk to me, baby. Please say something." She searched for the gunshot wound and found it right above his left hip.

Buck's eyes opened. "Katie," he murmured, "I love you, but I think I might need mouth to mouth." He tried to chuckle but winced in pain. Katie leaned over Buck, smiling and crying. Behind them, Sergeant Haskins led Tate away in handcuffs.

CHAPTER TWENTY-EIGHT

Vineyards and Victories

Katie looked at her bruised face in the mirror as she sat in Buck's hospital room. Despite having been shot, Buck only needed stitches, pain medication, and bedrest. Katie was discharged and told to stay hydrated after they'd examined her face and found no broken bones.

She and Randy were keeping Buck company when Sergeant Haskins stopped by to check on them. He tapped on the open door. "Katie?"

Katie turned around and smiled when she saw the sergeant.

"I thought I'd come talk to the girl who's been driving my whole town crazy lately," he said as he walked in.

"I guess that's me," she said, laughing. "Thanks for helping my dad and friends out, Sergeant Haskins. I really can't thank you enough. I don't even want to think of how this could've turned out."

He looked over at Buck. "Yeah, what Buck did wasn't the smartest, but it worked. I'm just glad that Tate was a lousy aim."

Buck's eyes were only half open. "Me too, Sarge. Me too," he managed.

They all chuckled. "So, Sergeant," Randy said, "what will become of Tate?"

"For now, he'll be arraigned and sent to jail," Sergeant Haskins said. "He'll probably be sentenced to quite a few years for the array of charges against him. Stalking, kidnapping, attempted murder, and harassing phone calls just to name a few. I don't think you'll have to worry about him ever again."

Randy smiled and sighed. "That's the best news I've heard in a long time. Now we can finally get our lives back together."

There was a knock at the door and Matt stuck his head in. "Katie, can I talk to you for a minute?" he said.

"Sure," she said, standing up. She walked over to Buck's bed and kissed him on the forehead. "I'll be back. Don't you go anywhere."

He reached out and took her hand as she turned to go. "Katie," he slurred, "I will never leave you, ever." She giggled and leaned over to kiss him, but he stopped her.

"What's wrong, Buck?"

"Oh, nothing," he said. "I just can't feel my lips right now, and I don't want to miss how great yours feel on mine."

She blushed and turned around, then walked outside with Matt. The early evening breeze was warm on her skin.

"They're going to be putting Tate away for a long time," she said as they walked along the sidewalk in front of the hospital.

"Yes, so I hear. I'm really glad about that, Katie. He'll be getting what he deserves." He rubbed the back of his neck.

Katie stopped and stood in front of Matt. "Thanks for coming out here, Matt. I know the letter I left was hurtful, and I feel so bad about running out on your parents like I did." She looked into his eyes.

"Well, their main concern was that you were all right, and they're glad you are. I showed Mom pictures of your face and what that animal did to you, and she said your new nickname should be Rocky." Matt laughed.

Katie grinned. "Tell her it's a deal."

"You know," Matt said, lowering his voice, "I was thinking about how I felt watching Buck standing out in front of that house, telling Tate to shoot him, and I gotta be honest with you. I don't know if I could've done that. That took a lot of guts on his part. He could've been seriously hurt or killed."

Hearing that rocked Katie to the core, and she knew then more than ever that she loved him. The mere thought of him no longer around shattered her heart.

"Yeah, you're right, Matt. It could've ended badly. I'm thankful for the fast actions of the police officer that tackled Tate."

"So, um," Matt said, "I'm going to head home now. My flight leaves soon, and Mom and Dad are anxiously waiting for me to come home. Mom said she has a friend she wants to set me up w—er, introduce me to, as she put it." He laughed.

Katie leaned in and gave him a hug. "I know you will go far, Matt. Thank you again for loving me and caring for me and making sure I was safe."

As they walked back to the main entrance, Randy came outside.

"Well, sir, I'm going to head out," Matt said, extending his hand.

Randy pulled him in for a hug. "Thanks for all you and your parents did for Katie and me. We really appreciate it."

Katie and Randy watched Matt drive away then walked back inside to be with Buck. A few hours later, Buck was discharged, and they all made their way home. Katie helped him out of the car and walked alongside him as he tottered toward the front door.

"Can we stop here for a minute?" Buck said as they reached the porch. "I want to take a break and sit out here in the rocking chair with you, Katie. Especially now without any fear someone is watching us."

"Of course, babe," Katie said, smiling. "That's a great idea."

Randy walked up behind them and helped Katie lower Buck into the chair. "How about some coffee, guys?" he asked as he walked toward the front door.

"Would you mind if I had hot cocoa instead, Dad?"

He laughed. "Sure, Peach, you can have anything you want."

A few minutes later, Randy walked back out with their mugs and sat down in the chair next to Buck.

"I don't even know what to say or where to begin, Buck," Randy said as tears welled up in his eyes. "The fact that you put your life on the line to save Katie's is just beyond words, beyond anything I have ever seen anyone do. I don't know how to repay you, son. I don't."

He chuckled. "A week or two off is all I ask, Boss."

"You got it, bud."

After several weeks, Katie felt much better, and the bruises had all but disappeared from her face. Buck looked better, too, and was able to get around faster, although he still hadn't returned to work.

Katie had fallen in love with the vineyard, flabbergasted at how quickly Randy had been able to pull it all together. They were almost ready for their first harvest to be sent to the winery.

"You know, Dad," Katie said as she sat on the sofa folding clothes, "I don't think I could be any happier than I am right now."

She held one of Buck's shirts to her face and took in its warmth and fresh scent. "I really do love him, Dad. I think I have all along but was just too stubborn to admit it." Katie folded the shirt and laid it on the back of the couch.

From the rocking chair across from her, Randy smiled and lifted his mug to take a sip of his coffee. "I knew it all along, Peach, but I couldn't be the one to tell you. That you had to figure out on your own. I knew he loved you as well. That became very clear to me while you were away."

"I know I shouldn't do this," she said, "but I keep replaying what happened over and over in my head." She stared at the trees outside the living room window. "I just don't want to imagine what could have happened."

Randy walked over to her and laid his hand on her shoulder. "I don't want to imagine what I would've done had your injuries been worse, Katie." He leaned over and kissed her cheek, then changed the subject. "So, what do you and Buck have planned?"

A smile grew on Katie's face. "He said he wants to take me out to the vineyard to watch the stars tonight," she said. She folded the last shirt and placed it in the clothes basket.

"That sounds like a lot of fun."

Katie's smile lingered. "Yes, it will be so romantic."

"Welp, I'm going to run over to Frank's to pick up dinner, Peach. You get some rest now." Randy picked up his wallet and keys and headed out.

Katie still hadn't worked up the courage to go back into Merriman's, even after all this time. Everyone understood why, though. Violet would set her up with beautiful bouquets and send them home with Randy from time to time. Frank, meanwhile, didn't take it personally. He knew one day she'd come back, just not now. It was still too fresh.

Buck came over just before dinner with a bouquet of fresh daisies he had picked just for her. She opened the door with a smile, and he reveled in her glow. The bruises were gone, and her face was more beautiful than it had ever been. He was so glad that she was safe and still in his life. He wanted it to be that way forever. He wrapped his free arm around her waist and pulled her close.

"I love you, Katie. Forever," he said, and kissed her soft, pink lips.

That evening, they feasted on steak and potatoes and Katie's homemade apple pie. After dinner, they sat around the table talking, laughing, and reminiscing. As darkness set in, Buck excused himself to gather what he needed to take his best girl out to see the stars.

Randy and Katie cleared the table and brought the dishes to the sink. After they'd washed and dried a few plates, Randy looked over at Katie and smiled. "You go outside, girl. I'll finish these up. Go have fun."

❧

Katie and Buck lay on a quilt in the lush, green grass near the fields. She rested her head on his outstretched arm and stared up at the sky, taking a deep breath and letting it out slowly. He turned his head and gazed at her soft, ivory complexion, her emerald-green eyes, her rich auburn hair. Buck felt like the luckiest man in the world to be able to be here with her on this perfect night.

"Is that the Big Dipper?" Katie asked, pointing to the sky.

He smiled. "I believe that is the Little Dipper, actually."

He rolled over onto one arm and admired the contours of her face, glimmering in the lights of the vineyard. Still looking skyward, she smiled to acknowledge that he was staring at her, and that turned into a chuckle and then an outright laugh. Then she rolled over and met his gaze, nose touching nose. "I bet you want to kiss me, don't you?"

He loved the twinkle in her eye. "Well, it does seem like the perfect timing for a kiss, wouldn't you agree?"

"You gotta catch me first!" Katie got up and took off running.

Laughing, he stood up and walked as fast as he could to catch up to her. Katie stopped and turned around, and just as Buck caught up, thunder crashed, and the skies let loose. In the blink of an eye, a popup rainstorm splashed the vineyard and surrounding fields. Katie held her arms outstretched to the sky, laughing even harder now that they'd been soaked to the bone almost instantly by this warm summer's rain.

He walked over to her and wrapped his arms around her petite waist. Face to face, eye to eye. He held her face in his hands as raindrops ran down her nose from her forehead. He kissed her.

His kiss was long and passionate. As rain fell hard around them, he stepped back, smiled, and got down on one knee. Katie gasped, then choked up. He pulled out a box from the pocket of his soaking-wet jeans.

His hands trembled as he opened it.

"Katie Calhoun, I have loved you since I first laid eyes on you," he said, staring up at her beautiful face. "You are my everything. I love your laugh, your heart, and your sweet spirit, and I just can't imagine my life without you in it. Please make me the happiest man alive. Will you marry me?"

Katie's heart pounded, and a mixture of tears and raindrops flowed down her face. It had been such a long journey, and she couldn't believe that after all the trials and heartache, she would actually get to have her happily ever after.

"Yes! Yes, Buck Brady, I will marry you!"

As he slipped the ring onto her finger, she looked down and realized it was her mother's ring. In that moment, she knew this was the best decision she could have ever made.

As the rain tapered off, Mars came bounding over to them from the barn. She was so glad he could have a home here instead of being sent to a shelter and suffering alone for the rest of his life. He was an older dog, and he needed a home where he would finally be loved.

Buck reached down and scratched his ears. "You can be the best man, buddy." He and Katie both laughed.

Desires of the heart can be achieved if and only if they are truly sought after. Go after your dreams and never stop reaching for the stars.